A PUFFIN BOOK

PROPERTY OF

_____

_____

D1078363

Sch

ANITA DESAI was born and educated in India. Her published works include adult novels, two collections of short stories and two books for children. She is a Fellow of the Royal Society of Literature in London and the Academy of Arts and Letters in New York. She is a Professor of Writing at the Massachusetts Institute of Technology in Cambridge, Massachusetts.

ANITA DESAI

The Village By The Sea

A PUFFIN BOOK

PUFFIN BOOKS

UK | USA | Canada | Ireland | Australia
India | New Zealand | South Africa

Puffin Books is part of the Penguin Random House group of companies whose
addresses can be found at global.penguinrandomhouse.com.

puffinbooks.com

First published by William Heinemann Ltd 1982
Published in Puffin Books 1984
Reissued in this edition 2015

001

Set in 12.5/16.5 pt by Sabon LT Std
Typeset by Jouve (UK), Milton Keynes
Printed in Great Britain by Clays Ltd, St Ives plc

A CIP catalogue record for this book is available from the British Library

ISBN: 978-0-141-35976-2

www.greenpenguin.co.uk

MIX
Paper from
responsible sources
FSC® C018179

Penguin Random House is committed to a
sustainable future for our business, our readers
and our planet. This book is made from Forest
Stewardship Council® certified paper.

For Lina, Aditi and Ranjit Mayadas whose
house in Thul provided me with many
holidays and all the material for this book

This story is based entirely on fact. Thul is a real village on the western coast of India and all the characters in this book are based on people who live in this village; only their names have been altered.

A few of the Indian words in this story will not be explained by their context and may be unfamiliar to young English readers. Often they have no direct English equivalent and I hope the following will therefore help you as you read.

Bai means mistress, or Mrs.
Bhai means brother.
A *chapati* is a flat disc of unleavened bread.
A *dhoti* is a garment worn by men in India, consisting of a piece of cloth wrapped around the lower half of the body and held at the waist.
Diwali is the name of the Hindu festival of lights.
Jai means victory.

A *jalebi* is a sweet made from sugar, flour and water.

A *lakh* is one hundred thousand.

Puja is a religious ceremony involving prayer.

Rangoli are decorative patterns drawn on the ground with white or coloured powders.

A *rupee* here is roughly equivalent to six pence.

ANITA DESAI

I

WHEN Lila went out on the beach it was so early in the morning that there was no one else there. The sand was washed clean by last night's tide and no one had walked on it except the birds that fished along the coast – gulls, curlews and sandpipers. She walked down to the sea with the small basket she carried on the flat of her hand, filled with flowers she had plucked from the garden around their house – scarlet hibiscus blooms, sweet-smelling spider lilies and bright butter-yellow allamanda flowers.

When she came to the edge of the sea, she lifted the folds of her sari and tucked them up at her waist, then waded out into the waves that came rushing up over her feet and swirling about her ankles in creamy foam. She waded in till she came to a cluster of three rocks. One of them was daubed with red and white powder. It was the sacred rock, a kind of temple in the sea. At high tide it would be inundated but now, at low tide, it could be freshly consecrated. Lila took the flowers from her basket and scattered them about the rock, then folded her hands and bowed.

Just then the sun lifted up over the coconut palms in a line along the beach and sent long slanting rays over the silvery sand to touch her on the back of her head. Enjoying their warmth, she stayed bowed for a little while, her feet still in the cold, whispering waves. The sun lit up the pink and mauve waves with sparkles. Far out, stretched along the horizon, was the fishing fleet that had been out all night, the sails like white wings, or fins, lifting out of the sea. They were anchored and still: they would not return before sundown.

Later in the morning more women would come and offer flowers at the sacred rock. Some would say a little prayer for the safety of the fishermen at sea because they were all the wives and daughters of fishermen. Some would simply bow, like Lila, and say a greeting to God. It seemed a good way to start the morning. There was no real reason why they prayed to this rock rather than any other rock, but they needed something to which they could offer flowers and red *kum-kum* powder as they said their prayers, and the large flat-topped one that stood in the shallow water and was easy to approach was the most convenient one. It was not so far away as the temple in the village at the far end of the beach, nor did they need to give money to a priest who would perform the *puja* for them. The women preferred to do it themselves.

When Lila's father still owned a boat and went to sea to fish, her mother used to bring flowers to this rock in the sea, and pray. But he no longer fished, he had sold his boat to pay his debts, her mother was too ill and weak to get out of her bed, and it was Lila who came to begin the morning with an offering of flowers to the sea. Sometimes she felt it was the best time of day for her, the only perfectly happy and peaceful one. Emptying out the last petals from her basket into the waves which quickly carried them away, she turned and walked back up the beach to the line of coconut palms now gilded by the sun. It was time to start work.

She climbed over the dunes that were spangled with the mauve flowers of seaside ipomea into the coconut grove and passed the white bungalow that was locked and shuttered. It belonged to rich people in Bombay who came only rarely for their holidays. Its name was written on a piece of tin and tacked to the trunk of a coconut tree: *Mon Repos*. What did that mean? Lila had never found out and she wondered about it every time she walked past it, up the path that led through the coconut grove.

The morning light was still soft as it filtered through the web of palm leaves, and swirls of blue woodsmoke rose from fires in hidden huts and mingled with it. Dew still lay on the rough grass and made the spiderwebs glitter. These webs were small and thickly matted and stretched across the grass, each with a hole in the centre to trap passing insects. Butterflies flew up out of the tussocks and bushes of wild flowers – large zebra-striped ones with a faint tinge of blue to their wings, showy black ones with scarlet-tipped wings, and little sulphur-yellow ones that fluttered about in twos and threes.

Then there were all the birds flying out of the shadowy, soft-needled casuarina trees and the thick jungle of pandanus, singing and calling and whistling louder than at any other time of the day.

Flute-voiced drongoes swooped and cut through the air like dazzling knives that reflected the sun and glinted blue-black, and pert little magpie robins frisked and flirted their tails as they hopped on the dewy grass, snatching at insects before they tumbled into the spider's traps. Pairs of crested bulbuls sang from the branches. A single crow-pheasant, invisible, called out 'coop-coop-coop' in its deep, bogeyman voice from under a bush, and a pigeon's voice cooed and gurgled on and on. It was the voice of the village Thul as much as the roar of the waves and the wind in the palms. It seemed to tell Lila to be calm and happy and all would be well and all would be just as it was before.

But when Lila came to the log that bridged the swampy creek and led to their hut on the other bank, she looked at the hut and knew that nothing was as it had been before, and nothing was well either. The hut should have been rethatched years ago – the old palm leaves were dry and tattered and slipping off the beams. The earthen walls were crumbling. The windows gaped, without any shutters. There was no smoke to be seen curling up from under a cooking pot on a fire, as in the other huts in the surrounding groves of coconut and banana.

Her two sisters, Bela and Kamal, stood at the door brushing their teeth with twigs they had broken off the neem tree at the back. They had not washed or changed for school. When she called to them, 'Why don't you dress? You'll be late for school,' they answered, 'But you haven't even made us our tea yet – *you're* late.'

Lila threw down the little basket at the door and went in to make a fire. She knew she ought to do it before she went to the beach. Then she could put on the pot of water and have it boiling when she came back. But somehow, when she woke up in the morning, she felt she had to flee to the beach: she couldn't face the dead ashes or the dirty cooking pots of the night before until she had been out on the beach and seen the sea and scattered flowers on the sacred rock. Now she had been there, she would collect firewood, light it and make tea for the family. She wished Bela and Kamal would understand.

She made them their tea silently, throwing a fistful of tea leaves and another of sugar into the pot of water on the smoking fire she had built. The three sisters sat on their heels, waiting for it to boil and for their brother to bring them some milk. Once they had had a buffalo but she, too, had been sold to pay debts. Now milk had to be bought from a cowherd in the village.

They sat on the threshold, looking down the path that led through the coconut grove and soon they saw Hari coming along with a small brass pot of milk in his hand – all they could afford. Unlike the two little girls, he had washed and was dressed in clean khaki shorts and a shirt. The small girls ran to take the milk from him, Lila poured some into the pot, and soon it was ready and they carried their metal tumblers of hot tea out to a string bed under the frangipani tree and sat there and sipped.

'What about Father and Mother?' asked Hari.

'I'll take Mother's glass to her,' said Lila.

'But Father's asleep,' said Bela and Kamal together.

Hari's head sank low as he stared at the empty tumbler while Lila pushed and shoved and made her sisters change into their indigo blue skirts and white blouses that all the schoolgirls in the village wore, and found their few tattered books with which they set off for school. Then Hari got up and said he would see them to school and stop in the field on his way back to do some digging and watering.

Lila went in with a tumbler of tea for her mother. She stopped to add a little extra milk to it. Then she went past the curtain in the doorway to the room where her mother lay on the string bed on some old grey sheets. She herself looked like a crumpled grey rag lying there. She had been ill for a long time. No one knew what was wrong. She had no pains and no fever but simply grew weaker and weaker all the time. Now she could not sit up to drink her tea. Lila had to lift her head and help her drink in little sips from the tumbler. She was very gentle and careful because her mother seemed so frail one hardly liked to touch her.

She also kept her head turned away from the heap that lay on a mat in a corner of the dark, shadowy room. The heap did not stir but made a grumbling sound of obstructed breathing and also stank. Lila could smell the fermented toddy even from a distance – it was a smell she had known and hated since she was a small girl. She kept her nose wrinkled up and wished her father would throw himself into some other corner to sleep and not foul her mother's room with the stench of drunkenness. But no one dared tell him, least of all her mother.

All she said was, 'Lila, have the girls gone to school?'

'Yes.'

'And Hari to the fields?'

'Yes, Hari to the fields.'

'Then you must sweep and go to market and cook, Lila.'

'Yes, Ma,' said Lila, although she did not need to be told. She had given up going to school long ago, so that she could stay home and do the cooking and washing and look after the others. She got up to start.

Bela and Kamal went running down the village road with their books, Hari following and pretending to drive them on with a switch.

The village road was a dusty lane that ran between groves of tall palms and even taller, slim, green betelnut palms. The houses along this road were not the thatched huts of the shore but solid bungalows of brick with wooden doors and iron grilles at the windows. Most of the verandas had swings hanging from their ceilings and on some old men sat dozing in the morning sun while a white cat slept on the floor and women sat on the steps, picking through trays of rice. In the yards hibiscus bushes bloomed and grubby chickens scratched in the dust. The post office was not open yet but the single shop that sold rice, wheat, sugar and kerosene was, and Bela and Kamal stopped outside it.

'Go on, go on, you're late,' Hari shouted, raising his switch.

'Hari-*bhai*, buy us sweets,' they chanted. 'Buy us a few sweets.'

'No sweets,' he shouted. 'I have no money.'

'Oh Hari-*bhai,* just three – only two – then one, just one,' they screamed, but Hari shook his head and frowned. They saw he was serious and walked on disappointedly.

At the edge of the village was a big pond. Here buffaloes stood knee-deep, drinking or bathing. Lotuses bloomed – crimson ones with crimson leaves and crimson stalks, and white ones with green leaves and green stalks. Ducks paddled between the large, flat, round leaves, and china-white egrets stood in the shallows, fishing. On the farther bank women were washing clothes and shouting and laughing as they beat the clothes on flat stones and sent up showers of water. They were dressed in bright pink and orange and lime-green saris which they had tucked up at their waists so that they could wade into the water and stand in the mud. They seemed to be enjoying this part of their housework.

Now the lane became dusty and rutted. Several children were running along – boys in khaki shorts and white shirts to the boys' school on the right of where the lane met the highway, and the girls in their indigo skirts and white blouses to the girls' school on the left, just below the low hill on which stood a temple. Hari used to go to the boys' school but lately he had stopped, saying he had to work in the fields now that their father did not even pretend to work any more. So he only came as far as the foot of the hill where Bela and Kamal turned towards their tin-roofed school in the middle of a bare, dusty field, and then turned to go back.

As he turned round, he saw the bright glint of a new tin shack that he had not seen before. It was just round the foot of the hill from the school – four walls made of sheets of corrugated iron and straw thatch for a roof. Outside it stood a yellow lorry with a load of steel pipes.

Hari was curious to see something new in the village just as all villagers were since there so seldom was anything new. Picking up a pebble to toss from one hand to the other, he walked towards it. There seemed to be no one around although the door was open and he could see a cooking fire and some tin pots on the earthen floor of the hut. He went to inspect the lorry and there found the driver asleep on the front seat, his bare feet sticking out of the window. Hari stared, wondering who could have sent these steel pipes and why. The man snored loudly.

Hari walked back to the lane and there met one of the village boys wheeling his bicycle through the dust.

'Hey, Ramu – who has come to build a house here?' he called to the boy.

Ramu stopped and waited till Hari had caught up with him. 'Haven't you heard?' he asked. 'Everyone is talking about it in the village.'

'I don't go to the village,' Hari said. 'All they do there is drink.' He did not add that he was afraid to meet his father outside the toddy shop, and that he did not have any money to spend in the village shops.

'But you must have heard,' Ramu said. 'The government is going to build a great factory here. Many factories. Hundreds of them.'

'*That* is going to be a factory?' Hari waved at the tin and straw shack left behind and laughed scornfully.

'Oh, that is only the watchman's hut. First they send a watchman. Then they send their materials so he can guard them. Soon they will be sending bulldozers and earthmovers and steamrollers. They are going to widen the highway – make it twice as broad. Then their machines can be brought here. Then they will build houses for the workers. The workmen will come. The factories will be built.'

Ramu went on and on describing the future to Hari who could not believe it. The tin shack and the yellow lorry with the sleeping driver did not look as if they could be the beginning of such mighty changes. 'And what will happen to the hill and the temple on top?' he asked, completely disbelieving Ramu's tale.

Ramu made a cutting gesture with his free hand, as if he were cutting through a swathe of grass. 'They will cut it down,' he said. 'Make it all flat. Build the factory on top.'

'Hah.' Hari laughed, not believing a word. How could the hill and the temple disappear? It had been there all his life and his father's and grandfather's as well. Ramu was surely telling a tale. 'We'll see,' he said. 'What are they going to make in this wonderful factory of yours?'

'It isn't mine – but they will give me work. They will have to have men working in their factories – so we will get jobs,' shouted Ramu, waving his arm in the air and looking excited.

Now they had come to the village pond where the lane became smooth and even. Ramu jumped on to his cycle and pedalled off, shouting, 'We'll get jobs, Hari – we'll get jobs. You'll see.'

Hari thought about it all morning while he worked quietly in the field behind their hut. All the time that he hoed and dug out stones and pulled up roots, preparing the single small field for a winter crop of vegetables, the same words kept ringing in his ears – 'A job. A factory. Many jobs. Many factories. Jobs – factories. Factories – jobs.' He was soon sweating in the sun as he bent and pulled and tugged and dug. Once he cut his big toe quite painfully on a sharp stone. Once, as he approached a sturdy ixora bush that had to be cut, he saw a black snake slither under it and hide so that he had to leave it alone. But all the time he thought of the factory and a job. Could he get one, too? Could he work in a factory and earn money? No, he thought, he had not finished school. Although he could read and write and add figures, he had not taken an exam and had no degree, so how could he get a job? But did you really need a degree to work in a factory? Any man could work machines and use tools if his hands were fit to work. As Hari's were.

He stopped to study his hands. They were worker's hands – square and brown and callused. It was true he had done nothing with them but dig and sow and break coconuts from the trees and drag nets in the sea, but he could teach them to work machines. He felt sure he could. Was he sure? No, perhaps not quite sure.

He was still standing and staring at his hands when Lila came down the path from their hut, a water pot held against her hip with one hand and Hari's lunch of a few dry *chapatis* tied in a cloth in the other, and their short black and white dog Pinto following at her heels. Pinto darted forwards when he saw Hari and came hurrying to meet him. Lila followed slowly. She was tired and she did not like to see Hari standing idle in the empty field. But she only said, 'Here – eat,' and handing him his lunch, went to the well to fill the water pot.

Hari followed her and helped her to draw up the bucket after it had plopped into the still green depths of the well, frightening a small frog or two, slowly filled and grown heavy at the end of the rope. Then he sat down on the edge of the well to eat his bread. There was nothing to eat with the *chapatis* but a pinch of salt and a few green chillies Lila had plucked from a bush near their hut.

She stood watching him, her hands on her hips.

'What will we do?' she said suddenly.

Hari knew exactly what she meant, but he did not like to tell her so. He did not feel like talking. He never did talk much and always preferred to think things out very slowly and carefully before he did. So he went on eating his dry bread and chillies.

'Father's still lying there, asleep. He sleeps all day. He will only get up at night and go straight to the toddy shop,' Lila said, almost crying.

'Let him,' said Hari.

'Hari, he will kill himself drinking the toddy those wicked men make and sell.'

'Let him,' Hari said again, chewing.

'And Mother? And Mother?' cried Lila. 'And us? What about us? Who will look after us?'

'*He* does not look after us,' said Hari, spitting out the end of a very sharp chilli. 'We look after ourselves, don't we?'

'But how?' cried Lila. 'We don't go to school any more, you and I. Only Bela and Kamal go – and next year we won't be able to buy them any new books. We hardly eat anything but this dry bread, or dry rice, every day. There's hardly ever any money to buy anything with in the bazaar – only when we sell our coconuts to the Malabaris. The only time we eat fish is when you go fishing. Father never does. And then, Mother: how will Mother get well if she never gets any medicine?'

Now Hari hunched his shoulders. He did not like Lila to say – to scream aloud – all these things that he knew and thought about all the time. What could he do? He worked in the field, he climbed the trees and brought down the coconuts to sell. When he had time, he took a net and fished along the shore. What more could he do? He knew it was not enough but it was all he could do.

'What can I do?' he mumbled. 'I'm doing what I can.'

'I know,' said Lila, with tears beginning to tremble in her eyes. 'But don't you think we have to do something *more* now, Hari?' she pleaded.

This made Hari stop chewing, put away the remains of his lunch and stare at her while he thought of a way to answer her and reassure her. 'Something will come along, Lila,' he said at last. 'The boys in the village say a factory is to be built in Thul and everyone will get jobs there. Perhaps I will get one too.'

'When?' cried Lila.

'I don't know. Not now, not for a long time. In the meantime – in the meantime I'll look for work. The next time the de Silvas come from Bombay I'll ask them if they can take me back with them and give me work.' This was an idea he had had but never spoken of before. He was quite surprised to hear the words out loud himself. So was Lila.

'In Bombay?' she cried. 'Then you would have to leave us, Hari?'

'Yes. If I am to stay here, I could get work on a fishing boat – I will ask and we'll see.'

Lila nodded. She felt relieved now to think Hari was growing up and would soon be able to find work and earn money. Of course he was still young, a year younger than her, and she could not expect him to work and earn like a man. Change would not come suddenly or quickly to their home and family, but it would come. She had to believe that it would come.

She got up and bent to pick up the heavy water pot. Hari bent too, to help, and together they lifted it on to her head. She stood for a moment to get her balance and then walked away, back to the hut. Now she could go back to work. Pinto followed her, just as he always did, devotedly.

Hari could not work any more. Although he had felt hopeful when talking to Lila of the future, he now wondered if he could really do anything about it. He stared at the dry, stony field that he had to plant with vegetables. What if he did clear and dig the field and sow some aubergines and marrows? The vegetables would be eaten. Then there would be nothing. It was simply not enough.

He walked down to the sea which was heavy and still and glittering in the noonday sun. The tide was far out. The fishing fleet stood becalmed at the horizon as if it had come to the end of the world and could go no further, its sails hanging slack at this still time of day. Only the pariah kites wheeled in the sky, up in the very dome of it, looking down on the crawling sea and the little creatures on earth from their great height and distance. Now and then they whistled thin, shrill whistles. And the pigeons cooed and cooed in the great banyan trees, sounding as if they were trying to console.

Hari sat down in the grove of casuarina trees where it was always shady and even a little breeze murmured through the soft grey needles of the old twisted trees. It was the coolest and shadiest spot on the whole beach and Hari was not the only one to seek it out at midday. One of the old men who owned the coconut grove next to theirs lay there asleep, his head on a pile of casuarina needles, his turban spread over his eyes. He was a bad-tempered, drunken old man and Hari was careful not to wake him.

He put his hands behind his head and leaned against a tree trunk, half closing his eyes against the glare from the sea. Out of the white-hot sky one of the floating kites swooped suddenly down, snatched up something on the beach and swooped upwards again. Hari opened his eyes to see what it was that dangled helplessly from its beak. A pair of kites chased after it, the prey dropped from its beak and Hari saw that it was a dead snake.

He was going to get up and go and inspect it when Ramu came cycling up and stopped under the trees, along with two other boys from the village who, like Hari, had given up going to school although not for the same reasons as Hari. He could no longer pay the fees, low as they were, nor buy books which they could easily for their fathers owned fishing boats and went out to fish and brought home catches they could sell to the dealers who took them to Bombay in lorries. They had simply grown bored with school and were waiting for some opportunity to come along which would bring them money and a good time. They were quite old enough to help their fathers fish but they did not like to, thinking it a boring occupation for uneducated men.

Hari, Ramu, Bhola and Mahesh – they used to play on the beach together and go hunting with their dogs, and wrestle and climb coconut trees and go to the occasional stage shows that were put on in the village on festival nights. Now they were too old to play and they just sat or lay about under the casuarina trees, talking.

What did they talk about?

'We will get jobs – then we will have money.'

'*How* will we get jobs?' Hari asked, sitting up suddenly and filling his hands with fistfuls of sand. 'They will bring men from the cities to work in the factories.'

'No, they won't,' all three boys shouted in protest.

They were silent for a minute, then one said, 'How can they? City people won't come to live in a village. Where can they live? There's nowhere for them to live, and no shops, no cinema. They won't want to come here. We live here – we can work in their factories.'

'We don't know how to,' Hari said.

'As if we can't learn!'

'Anyone can learn.'

'Anyone can work machines. They will show us – then we will do it.'

'We don't know anything about machines,' Hari protested. 'We only know how to fish and how to grow coconuts.'

'We will learn!' they shouted.

'How can we? We haven't even finished school, we know nothing,' Hari said, with disgust and despair lining his young face and darkening his black eyes. 'You have to go to college to learn – learn engineering.'

'College,' they scoffed. 'College and school teach you nothing. Books don't teach you to work machines. We will learn in the factories.'

'What factories are they? What will they make?' Hari asked, trying hard to be optimistic like them and stop feeling so worried and afraid.

But they could not answer.

'I think – I think cycles.'

'Someone said – motor cars.'

'See, you don't know,' Hari said angrily. 'You don't know anything.'

Ramu threw a coconut shell at him. Hari caught it and threw it back. It hit Ramu on the knee. He jumped up with a howl. The sleeping man woke up and roared at them. Ramu got up and ran. Hari chased him for a bit – then stopped – it was too hot to run. Hari went out on to the beach by himself.

He had seen Bela and Kamal, back from school, coming down the beach, each carrying a small brass pot and a little sickle knife in her hand. He knew they were going down to the rocks to chip at barnacles – Lila must have told them to collect molluscs for dinner. He would not join them – the exposed rocks along the beach were already crowded with women and girls, all pick-pick-picking at the barnacles with their small sharp *koytas* to dig out and collect the molluscs in them. It was an occupation for women. He turned away and decided to go and fetch his net and fish.

Bela and Kamal, in their indigo blue school skirts, crouched on the rocks and picked at them with their *koytas,* digging out the little slimy molluscs from the hard barnacle shells and slipping them into the little brass pot Lila had given them to fill. Many of their school friends chipped and cut beside them, as did some of their mothers and grandmothers. Others were burying baskets of palm fronds deep into the sand where the sea would cover them up and soften them, to be dug out several months later and worked into ropes. Now that the weather was cooler, it was pleasant to work out in the sun on the beach. They were just like the gulls and curlews and reef herons that stalked the shallows, fishing together, although – unlike the birds – they could not keep quiet and chattered and gossiped.

'Look, there goes Hema with her mother,' said Bela, pointing at two colourful figures on the beach – the mother dressed in a sari printed with bright flowers, purple and pink and orange, and the girl in a violet dress with a silver fringe.

Many of the women stared at their dazzling clothes and sniggered.

'They've been to Alibagh to buy fish.'

'Too fine to catch their own, eh?' said another.

'They don't need to. You know Biju – when he comes back from his fishing trip, he has tons of fish in his boat, tons and tons – prawns and pomfret and *surmai* and everything. They don't need to buy any fish.'

'Of course not – they *sell* it, they have so much.'

'In Bombay, where you get double the price you would here in Thul or even in Alibagh.'

'Twice? *Thrice* the price.'

'That's why they have all those gold bangles,' said one child, enviously.

For a while all the women were silent and one could hear only their *koytas* chipping at the barnacles encrusted on the rocks, and the jingle of their glass bangles as they chipped. All the women in Thul loved bangles and although few could wear gold or even silver ones, all had dozens of glass bangles – blue and green and gold, covering their arms from their wrists to their elbows, nearly. Bela and Kamal had far less, only six or eight each, which they had bought last Diwali at the fair. Glass bangles were cheap but did not last long, alas: they broke so easily but were pretty while they lasted.

Then one of the old grey-haired grandmothers, Kashi-*bai*, squatting on the rocks beside them, said, 'And have you heard – Biju is going to build yet another boat?'

'Another boat? But he has so many – why should he want one more?' the other women chorused.

'It is to be bigger and faster than all the others. My man told me the other day, he had it from Biju himself – this boat is going to have engines, so they can go out in all weathers, as far as Saurashtra and Gujarat. They will go far out to fish – far, far out where there is still plenty to catch. Over here there is not enough left.'

'No,' they agreed, 'not enough left, so little left.'

'Still, *our* men find fish here,' one women said. '*Ours* still fish here and find some.'

'But so little,' sighed the others. 'They bring home so little.'

Now Bela and Kamal were silent. Both were thinking, 'At least your men bring home a little. Our father does not even go fishing. Hari has to fish with just a net. And he can catch hardly anything at all.' They did not say this. Instead, they crawled about on the rocks, prising open the little lids of the barnacles, scooping out the molluscs and filling their small brass pot as best they could.

In the silence of the late afternoon, with the tide out and the breeze still, they all heard a sound that was like a whisper or a sigh, a deep sigh uttered by the ocean itself. Then the sigh extended into a long rustling, rippling sound. It came from far out at sea. The ripple lifted itself out of the flat, dull ocean – a long, white line that lifted and rippled and rushed closer and closer to land till it dashed against the rocks in a shower of spray. The tide had turned. It was coming in now. Along with it came the evening breeze, fresh and cool and lovely. Tide and breeze both rushing at them now, the women stopped work and got up. 'Time to go home,' they said, 'time to start the dinner,' and they collected their sickles and brass pots and started walking up the beach in twos and threes, the women in their bright green and orange saris and the girls in their blue and white school clothes, some chattering and laughing, others hobbling silently along.

Hari had seen them go as he brought his fishing net down the beach. He did not like to be watched, the only boy in the village with no boat and no job on the fishing boats. Also, he knew he could not hope to catch much in his net along the shore.

Still, he enjoyed it. He lowered his net into the surf and walked along, letting the coffee-coloured waves surge through it, and then dragged it out on shore. All he ever caught were a few gold and silver fish, too tiny to bother to pick up, gasping and swelling up as they puffed for air before they died. And three or four crabs – again too small to have any meat on them. He watched them lying on their backs and kicking their transparent legs in the air. A large black crow came hopping along to see what it could find. Hari amused himself by turning the crabs right side up so they could scuttle away down into the sea and safety. But the crow kept turning them over on to their backs again with its beak. Finally Hari left the crow to it and walked on with his empty net.

The fishing fleet was coming in. The first boat was already close to the shore, within shouting distance, and no sooner had a fisherman on board shouted than a horde of women came streaming down the beach from the village by the creek. All were carrying baskets. Some couldn't wait for the boats to come to shore and plunged into the sea, with their saris tucked up at their waists, and waded out to the boats. The fishermen lowered heavy baskets of fish down to them. They set them on their heads and came wading back to shore. Two or three of the fishermen followed them. The boats would not be able to come up the creek till the tide was high.

Now all was loud and noisy on the beach where it had been so still and quiet before. The fishermen began to auction off the baskets of fish. The women poked into them and spilled out the contents on to the sand. There were mounds of pink prawns, still crawling and alive, long snake-like 'Bombay duck', little flat shining pomfrets that really should have been left in the sea to grow, some blue-black speckled *surmai* that is so delicious to eat, and a few large black crabs. The women became louder and noisier as they fought over the baskets, pushing each other out of the way as they bid for the catch.

'Fifty rupees!' shouted a woman who had found a basket with some really large pomfrets that would fetch ten rupees each in Bombay, and the freshest, pinkest prawns. But 'Sixty rupees!' bawled another. 'Seventy!' shouted the third, a great, heavy woman wrapped in a purple sari, and when the other women hesitated, she opened up a loose cloth belt at her waist, removed a bundle of filthy notes from it and handed it over to the pleased, grinning fisherman. Bending to collect her basket, she hallooed loudly while the other women grumbled and bickered over the smaller baskets of fish.

In answer to her ringing halloo, a tonga came rattling down the beach. The brown mare's legs scissored along at great speed, the big wheels spun over the wet and glassy shore, the tonga-driver raised his whip and cracked it in the air, and the tonga went right through the surf and out of it till it reached the band of women and their baskets.

Again the bargaining began.

'Two rupees to the highway bus stop,' offered one woman who had bought a bag of prawns.

'Three rupees!'

'Five!'

But again the large woman who had so much money tied in her belt won. 'Six,' she said flatly, and without waiting for an answer from the tonga-driver, she climbed in with the basket. The tonga creaked, the horse staggered, but the tonga-driver set his cap at an angle, cracked his whip and set off at a trot up the sandy path along the creek to the highway where the woman would sell the fish to a lorry driver come to collect fish from the villages, or else get into the bus and go to Alibagh bazaar to sell it herself. The other women bickered over what was left, and Hari turned away – there was nothing more to watch.

He wished he could have bought one of those fish for his family. Better still, he wished he could have caught one. But his net was empty. He trailed it behind him as he walked back in the soft mauve twilight, whistling to himself.

Now the surf was rushing up around the rocks that Lila had scattered with flowers that morning. Soon the red and white powder sprinkled on it would be washed away, and the petals that stuck to it, too. Next morning someone would come and scatter more.

Up on the grassy bank where the path came down from their hut, Bela and Kamal were still skipping and playing. They were playing 'Lame'. Bela was hopping on one leg and trying to catch Kamal who was running about on two in a small square marked with pebbles. Bela lurched forward to catch her sister by the skirt, Kamal stepped aside and Bela fell on her knees.

'Don't roar,' Hari said, climbing up the bank. 'You weren't hurt.'

'I wasn't going to,' said Bela, getting up and dusting her knees.

'Look how dusty you've made your skirt,' said Hari.

'Lila will wash it.'

'Hmm – Lila has to do everything.'

'Have you caught any fish?' Bela asked quickly, to change the subject.

They could see his net was empty. 'You took home some molluscs, didn't you?' he asked.

Now Pinto came running down the path as if to call them before it was quite dark. The shadows from the coconut grove had spread all over the beach now, only the deep rose and orange glow of the sun in the west did not fade but grew more vivid and intense. The evening star was already out in the sky, the calm and radiant Venus, brighter even than the moon which was quite pale by comparison, a disc of milky white floating in the deep blue-black sky. As it grew darker, the moon and the star grew brighter.

'Pinto! Pinto!' Kamal called, running up the path towards him.

Pinto had been named after the man from whom they had taken him as a pup. He had come to the village to 'do business'. No one knew quite what his business was. He lived in a hut behind the ration shop with a dog for company, cooking for himself, strolling about the village and talking to people. He had become friendly with some of the men at the toddy shop, including their father, and asked him if he would like to go to Goa to work on the barges that carried iron ore from the mines down the river to the ships at sea. Their father thought he would like to go to Goa where the toddy was supposed to be especially fine, and he paid the man fifty rupees as his bus fare. Then, the day before they were to leave, along with several other jobless men from the village, Mr Pinto disappeared. Their father could not believe it, and sat stunned at the toddy shop all day. Coming home from school, Kamal heard the dog and the puppies crying in the deserted hut and picked up the smallest and weakest of them to take home. That was all they had in return for their father's fifty rupees. Later they learnt of many other men who had been duped by the man Pinto.

Of course no one could hold that against his dog or its puppies. Pinto was small and furry, black and white, and brave as a lion. He loved Kamal who had rescued him, but he was most devoted of all to Lila who stayed at home all day with him and never deserted him. Only Hari never touched him and looked at him accusingly always. Every time he saw Pinto he was reminded of his father's foolishness. Of course many other men in the village had been fooled as well. In fact, it had happened before – clever tricksters from the city coming and duping the ignorant villagers. It maddened Hari to think about it. He was not clever but he was not going to be fooled.

He followed the dog and the two girls slowly up the path, past the ghostly white walls of *Mon Repos* to their own hut where a lamp was lit and Lila was cooking their dinner.

Dinner was a hot curry made mainly of chillies and the few molluscs that the girls had collected floating in the red gravy, and some of the coarse, thick rice that they bought cheaply in the village shop.

Lila carried a plateful in to their mother and then sat on the kitchen floor and ate with her sisters and brother while Pinto waited quietly for the leftovers.

'Where's Father?' Hari asked in a low voice. 'Gone out?'

Lila nodded. They both felt relieved that he should be out of the house and disgusted because they knew he had gone to the toddy shop to drink all night with the other village drunkards.

Late at night Lila and Hari who were still awake heard the men coming home – their father and the three brothers from the neighbouring farm who drank together every night. The moon had set and it was deeply, intensely dark. The brilliant, flashing stars lit up the sandy beach but their light did not filter through the close-woven palm leaves in the grove where it was black as pitch. The men had had a lantern with them when they set out from the village but it had fallen and broken as they bumped into each other and into the tree trunks. They had laughed when it smashed and tinkled to bits on the stones, it was their wives who would think of the cost of a new lantern and more oil and wail bitterly over the loss. Now they tried to find their way home in the dark, calling to each other and singing to keep up their spirits.

They made so much noise that all the stray dogs of Thul woke up on hearing them and howled in alarm and protest.

Lila and Hari, who knew their father was among them, tried to shut out the sounds by covering their heads with their pillows. Lila hated and feared the noise so much that she cried to herself. Hari did not cry but he bit his lip and thought, 'Maybe a poisonous snake will bite him. He may step on one and be bitten, there are so many of them and it is dark. Then he would die.' He did not say that in fear, he said it with hope, as if he wished that was what would happen.

A little later there was a thump against the front door. Their father flung it open, jarring the whole house so that the walls shook and the palm-leaf thatch rustled. Pinto got up and gave a sharp yelp of alarm. Their father hissed at him, then bumped and lurched his way into their mother's room. They heard her begin to say something in protest, but he growled at her, then fell down in a heap and snored.

There was silence then. But the silence was not calm and lovely, it was full of fear and anger and nightmares.

2

LILA would go to the market at Thul today. She had to buy rice and perhaps some sugar and tea. Hari had brought down six bunches of coconuts and sold them to the Malabaris who came from Bombay in a lorry, so she had some money to spend. After Bela and Kamal had left for school, she took out her best sari from the green tin trunk in the corner of the room she shared with her sisters, and wore that. It was pink and had a pattern of brown flowers on it, and a border of violet. It was quite a cheap cotton sari but she wore it so seldom that it still looked fresh and new, and made her look so much younger and prettier than when she was dressed in an everyday sari which was always either dark green or dark purple, a single unpatterned colour, of thick cloth that stood much wear and tear. She herself felt younger and happier, and she took the market bag off its nail on the kitchen door and called goodbye to her mother who seemed to be asleep and did not answer, then set off down the beach that was brilliant with morning light and already hot.

A few other women were walking along to market with big black umbrellas to shield them from the white, blinding sun. The whole sea glittered with reflected light – it was like a mirror broken into bits and shining. Only the two small rocky islands of Undheri and Kundheri made two blobs in all that brightness. One of them had a small fort built long ago and empty now except for lizards. There was a breeze and the big dhows and catamarans swooped along as swiftly as birds, carrying their cargo up the coast to Gujarat and Saurashtra.

There was some commotion on the beach where a lorry had come and unloaded some timber. Now it was stuck in the sand. The driver was cursing loudly. Some of the village boys, the ones who did not go to school, came to help. They were spreading palm leaves on the sand under the wheels and trying to push the lorry out of the ruts on to them.

As Lila walked past, the wheels churned and threw up sand, then the lorry heaved and roared and was on its way.

'Next time, send your timber in a bullock cart,' one of the boys shouted after the driver and they all hooted and laughed.

'You think I would drive a bullock cart?' the driver shouted at them from the window.

'Bullocks don't stick in the sand like your fancy motor,' they screamed, but he was gone.

Lila did not stop to listen to more but hurried on, the soles of her feet burning on the hot sand. Then she came to the great banyan trees and the feathery-leaved drumstick trees that threw some shade on to the flat parched earth around the village and here it was cooler.

The village road leading to the market was lined with houses, some of them of solid brick and whitewashed, with bright floral patterns painted on their veranda walls, and others made of mud, with tattered palm leaves for roofs. But large or small, rich or poor, each had a sacred basil plant growing in a pot by the front door. Children and mongrels were playing in the dust, women were cleaning rice or throwing out pails of dirty water into the lane.

At the end of the lane was the temple. It was not very old or beautiful, it had four brick pillars supporting a tiled roof, an unwalled court and a small alcove that housed an idol. That was all. But there were several young men on the steps, sitting and playing drums and singing.

Lila could not help staring, and a young girl who was watching from a brick house across the lane called to her, 'See, Lila, the actors have come. They are going to do a play tonight.'

Lila smiled and went up to her friend Mina. 'Which play? Do you know?'

'I don't know, but it will be the same they always have of course,' said Mina who had seen them all, living as she did across from the temple where they were always staged. 'It will be the Radha-Krishna story, or the Rama-Sita, or the Nala-Damayanti. They always do those, you know.'

Lila had been to very few. 'Will you go and see it?' she asked enviously.

'I will sit on my veranda and see!'

'You're lucky to live here, in the village.'

'Come and watch it with me.'

'I can't come out at night.'

'Why not? Hari can bring you.'

'Hari and I can't go out together and leave the little girls alone.'

'What can happen to them? Your mother and father are there.'

But Lila shook her head without explaining. 'I have to go and buy some rice and sugar. Will you come?'

Mina had nothing to do, it seemed – her parents were trying to find her a husband – and she came. They strolled down the lane together, past the women who sat on the two sides of it, each with a banana leaf spread out before her on which she placed her wares – usually just a few shining purple aubergines, a bunch of spinach, five or six bananas, maybe a green coconut or two, and always handfuls of flowers, pink and white and yellow flowers plucked from the hedges and bushes. Mina bought some to make a garland for her hair. For a little more money, you could buy a ready-made one.

Lila could not spend money on such things. She went to one of the two grocery stores on the market square where one could buy rice, eggs, potatoes, sugar, oil, tea and sweets, and bought her rice there after carefully fingering all the varieties and choosing what seemed best at the lowest price.

There were many others waiting to be served. As they stood about, picking potatoes out of the buckets or trickling rice through their fingers, they gossiped. Lila and Mina learnt what the timber on the beach was for.

'Did you see, Biju's timber has come from Alibagh?'

'Oh, that was Biju's timber? For the boat?'

'And the diesel engine? Has that come too?' Someone sniggered.

'They will come – you'll see. Biju is not fooling us. He can buy *two* diesel engines with all his money.'

'We'll see.'

Lila and Mina turned back. Lila's shopping bag was full and heavy.

'My father says Biju has made all his money by smuggling.'

'Smuggling?' Lila was not really as surprised as she sounded. She had heard this before. 'Do you believe that?'

'Of course I believe it. How else could he have a television set in his house?'

'It doesn't work, Hari says, because we are too far away from the TV station in Bombay.'

'Perhaps they will go away to Bombay – when they've made enough money.'

Lila and Mina had never been further than Alibagh, the district headquarters two miles away. But they had heard of more adventurous people getting into the bus on the highway or the ferry at Rewas and going all the way to that great city across the sea. When they were smaller, they used to play at 'going to Bombay', but that would not do any longer.

Now Lila turned out of the village lane on to the beach, and it was more bare and white and blazing hot than before.

'Come at night to see the play,' Mina called after her.

'Perhaps,' Lila called back, knowing that she would not.

Now Biju's boat was being built. The village children – Hari often amongst them – would come and stand in groups of three and four to watch. Biju had got workmen from Alibagh to build his boat, he did not think the villagers at Thul could do it although they had been building boats all their lives. So the villagers liked to watch the Alibagh workers and to jeer at them. Sometimes that made Biju so angry that he shouted at them. It was always noisy.

Biju would come waddling down to watch the work in progress. A small boy would carry a folding chair down to the beach from his house and plant it on the sand for Biju to sit on. Biju would lower himself on to it very gingerly, twitching up his loose *dhoti* and sitting down very uncomfortably. He would obviously have been more comfortable squatting on his heels in the sand as the others did, but now that he was such a great ship-owner, he felt he had to sit on a chair unlike the rest of them.

Sometimes his wife came waddling down from the house to watch, too. She did not have a folding chair to sit on so she would stand till she got tired and went back to the house. It was a big, double-storeyed brick one set in a huge, gloomy estate of coconut and betelnut palms, grown so closely together that no light filtered through the leaves. Everywhere were signs of their wealth – they had several deep wells, many bullock carts, a row of bullocks, hens and ducks, piles of firewood, a pigeon house and the famous television set – the only aerial in Thul perched on the blue tin roof of their house. The house had its name painted in big crimson letters on a tin signboard: *Anand Bhavan*, House of Joy. But because of the closely planted trees and the lack of light and the untidiness of the big yard it looked more gloomy than joyful. Certainly Biju's wife trailed back to it slowly without any expression of joy. She knew how the villagers gossiped about them and she did not like it.

Almost the whole village stopped to watch the big boat being built at some time or the other. No one else owned such a large boat or even worked on one. Perhaps they were jealous and that was why no one had a good word for it. Or perhaps they really did not believe it would do well at sea being so large and clumsy and built by those Alibagh workmen at that. But in a way they were proud, too, that someone in Thul was able to build such a thing, even if it was Biju who everyone knew was dishonest and perhaps a smuggler.

'Smuggler, smuggler, smuggler,' children whispered behind their hands while they watched, and giggled till Biju roared at them and made them fly.

'Biju will go to jail! Biju will go to jail!' they sang as they ran, and he was much too fat and old to catch them and beat them as they deserved.

'Do you think we have smugglers in our village, Hari?' Bela and Kamal asked at night when they were lying in bed, not quite asleep.

'Of course we do.'

'What do they smuggle?'

'Silver and gold.'

'No – o – o!'

'Yes, of course. That's how they get so rich.'

'Where do you think they get it from – the silver and gold? Can you find it in the sea?'

'No, sillies, it's brought from foreign countries that have gold and silver mines and where it is cheaper than here. It is brought in dhows from Africa, from Arabia – and unloaded into fishing boats that go out to meet them in the sea. It's put into the smugglers' boats and brought to shore, and sold here for much money.'

'You've never seen that.'

'No,' Hari admitted, 'I haven't, but we've all heard about it. All you women love gold and silver jewellery so much, and buy such a lot of it, so the smugglers make a lot of money. Biju is supposed to make his money that way.'

'They say he's going to build the biggest fishing boat in Thul.'

'It will be the best one, too. I wish I could get a job on it.'

'Do you? On Biju's boat?'

'Yes, why not?'

'Oh, don't work for Biju, Hari. You just said he's a smuggler. He may turn you into a smuggler too.'

'Then I'll be rich, like him,' Hari chuckled, 'and buy you gold necklaces and silver toe-rings.'

But, 'Oh no,' they cried in alarm. 'The police will catch you and put you in jail.'

'Then they will take me to Bombay. At least I will get to Bombay.'

'Do you want to go away to Bombay?' they whispered, frightened by his bitter tone.

'Of course I do, don't you?'

They began to whisper to each other – they shared a bed – and a little later, when they heard a low groan from their mother in her room, Hari hushed them and they fell silent and were soon asleep.

While Hari lay awake, listening to their deep, even breathing and the deeper, louder breathing of the sea outside, he thought about the boats that sailed there so freely and could go to Bombay, to Africa, to Arabia if they liked. If only he could sail away in one of them – even if only to Bombay.

Bombay! He stared out of the window at the stars that shone in the sky and wondered if the lights of the city could be as bright, or brighter. It was a rich city: if he could get there, he might be able to make money, bring home riches, pieces of gold and silver with which to dazzle his sisters.

No! he told himself, closing his eyes. That was a foolish dream. He could not afford dreams, he must be practical and think out a scheme. That was not easy and the effort made him tired so that he gave up and fell asleep.

Instead of trying to net fish along the shore or digging in the arid field, Hari spent more of his time now standing with the other village boys and watching the work on the boat. The rough timber was being planed – the planks glowed in the sun, red-gold. It was good timber, not the coconut tree trunks they used themselves, but real wood, beautiful wood. It did not smell of the fish and the sea as everything else in the village did, but of timber, sawdust, forests, distant and wonderful things – dry, lasting, valuable. The smell of it made Hari's nostrils tingle.

Biju sat uncomfortably on his folding chair and watched, too. When anyone came near enough for him to address, he would boast about it. 'It is going to have a diesel engine and also a refrigerator. A deep freeze,' he pronounced slowly, more impressed than anyone else by the unfamiliar words. 'Then the boat can sail for six days and the catch can be put in the deep freeze and it will not spoil. It will still be fresh when it is taken to Bombay.'

'Frozen, not fresh,' Hari murmured, but Biju did not hear.

'How much will it cost, Biju?' asked one awe-struck villager who owned nothing but two goats and a cooking pot and could not picture the amount of wealth that Biju commanded.

'Oh, two *lakhs* – two and a half *lakhs,* maybe,' Biju said, trying to be casual about it, but rolling his eyes in horror at the expenditure.

'So much!'

'It doesn't matter. Once it is on the sea, it will fetch me fifty thousand rupees a day, at least,' Biju said, proudly.

Hari drew pictures in the sand with his toe as he stood listening. He really could not picture that amount any more than the simple goatman could, although he had spent a few years at school. He, too, was dazzled by the picture Biju drew of the future even if he did not quite believe in it. There was too much danger at sea, too much risk. He knew how many men lost their lives at sea, how many were drowned each monsoon, how many boats were wrecked and never came back at all. At the same time the thought of sailing far, far out to sea and never coming back or else only with riches untold, attracted him strongly.

When Ramu came by on his cycle and said, 'Hey, Hari, come with me,' he turned and went with him, plodding along in the deep, hot sand, wondering whether to side with Biju or with those who disbelieved Biju.

Ramu certainly did not believe him. 'It's only a fishing boat,' he said, 'even if it will have a deep freeze. You know what the monsoon is like – one storm and the boat will go smash like a matchbox, just like all the other boats. It won't be strong enough to sail during the monsoon, so what's the use? It's just bogus.'

'He will make a lot of money during the fishing season anyway,' said Hari.

'And what will he do when the fishing season is over? Sit on the beach and mend nets like all the other old men? No, it's better to have a job, to earn daily wages. And then there are all the other benefits – free lunch in the canteen, a doctor to see to you if you're ill, paid holidays – that's the life.' Ramu rang his bicycle bell loudly and cheerfully.

'And you think you can get a job like that in Thul?' Hari sounded doubtful, even more doubtful than he had been about the greatness of Biju's boat.

'Of course! Let the factory come up, Ramu will be the first in the line for a job,' Ramu shouted and rang the bell again, so loudly that a pair of egrets sitting on the back of a buffalo and picking at its ears took fright and flew off into the coconut grove for shelter.

'I will have a try, too,' Hari said. 'That's what I'll do, too.'

He saw now that there were two or three possibilities. Even if all he could do now was to fish and sell coconuts, later on he would be able to choose between a factory job, a job on a big fishing boat like Biju's or a job in Bombay if someone helped him to get there. Although it excited him to think that life held so many possibilities, it also frightened him. The men in Thul had never had to make such choices; they had never had to consider anything beyond fishing and farming along these shores. Now that was not enough. Hari saw that like Biju, although on a different scale, he would have to make a choice no one else in the village had made before. How? Who would help him? He walked along silently, worrying.

He would have gone on worrying and worrying in this way if an unexpected distraction had not arrived in the form of a heavily loaded car bumping over the grassy bank, dodging between the coconut trees and raising a cloud of dust in the narrow path before it came to a standstill in front of *Mon Repos,* the white bungalow that stood empty most of the year. It was the de Silvas, the family that came from Bombay to spend an occasional holiday in it and bring it suddenly to life for a few days. They had bought *Mon Repos* a year ago from the Vakils who had been one of the first Bombay families to build holiday cottages on the Thul beach. But they had grown too old and frail to come often and, after the house had stood empty for several years, sold it to the de Silvas who were young and energetic and seemed heartily to enjoy life on the beach. Whenever they came, life changed for the family in the little hut, too. Immediately there was a hubbub, all kinds of excitements and expectations, and of course work to be done, employment to be had, and wages.

Hari, Bela and Kamal stood by their door under the frangipani tree, tense with excitement, watching and holding Pinto back as he barked at the unfamiliar sight of a car and strangers till his voice was quite hoarse. There was a commotion in the marshy creek that separated the hut from the house, too – herons, egrets, kingfishers and moorhens all flapping into the dense greenery of the pandanus, the casuarina and the *bhindi* trees for shelter.

'Do you think they have come here for good?' Bela whispered.

'Hunh – who would live here if he had a house in Bombay?' Hari scoffed.

'But look how much luggage they've brought – it can't be just for a few days,' Bela said, and it was true that an unbelievable number of boxes and bags and baskets were being taken out of the car, out of the boot and off the luggage carrier so that anyone would have thought they had come to stay for ever.

Seeing the visitors staggering towards the house with their bags, Hari went to help. They carried all the baggage into the veranda and Hari went back to the hut, but one of the children from the house came running down the path to call him back.

When Hari went up the veranda steps he saw Mrs de Silva standing there, dressed in an outlandish costume unlike anything worn by the women in Thul and really not very much of it either so that Hari had to cast his eyes down and not look. She held out a basket and some money and asked Hari to go and buy some fish from the market. 'It must be very fresh,' she said over and over again. 'And we will want milk in the morning, and eggs. Can you get some – very, very fresh?' Hari had run errands like these for them before, whenever they had come for a weekend during this past year, but she always seemed to forget or else not to recognize him. City people had poor memories, Hari thought, or perhaps they saw so many hundreds of faces in the streets every day that they could not tell one from the other. But he only nodded and took the money and the basket from her and set off.

The next few days he was kept busy by them, buying their fish on the beach when the fishing fleet came in, and fetching eggs and milk from the village market. He also fetched bottles of soda water for their drinks in the evening when they liked to sit outdoors under the palms, on the metal folding chairs they had brought with them from Bombay, and sip at drinks.

They had brought their servants along, too – a cook who made their meals for them, and an ayah who washed their clothes and herded the smaller children down to the beach, carrying their towels and buckets and spades for them. It was a sight to see them all playing and splashing in the sea, screaming and laughing as the waves tumbled them over and the surf washed over their heads. Hari and his sisters watched discreetly from behind the bushes and the shrubs in the grove, but the Thul villagers walking up and down the beach on their errands stopped to stare and laugh. The people of Thul went into the sea to launch their boats or catch fish, not to swim and splash like fish or frogs. They thought the visitors from Bombay definitely touched in the head.

Although they did nothing but play or lie around and rest, everyone else around them was kept very busy. The cook and the ayah were not able to cope with all the work and Hari was engaged to help. (Earlier, his father had worked for them.) The cook made Hari cut and clean the fish when he brought it in and sometimes chop and slice the vegetables as well. The ayah asked him to sweep the house, so full of sand and spider webs after being shut and empty all this time. Then Hari had to call Lila to help. Lila tucked up her sari, fetched her broom and came to sweep. The children followed her about, fascinated by her glass bangles and the flowers she wore in her hair. When she stopped sweeping to smile at them, they came closer to admire her finery. They themselves wore no jewellery although they had enough clothes to change every day and sometimes twice a day. She promised to bring them flowers for their hair, too, and they followed her down the path to her hut.

'Kamal, Bela – come and make them some garlands,' she called to her sisters who had shyly wrapped themselves around the veranda posts as they watched them come. They unwrapped themselves, giggling, and went to collect jasmine.

The children took the garlands home to show their mother.

Next day when Lila came to sweep the house for them, she took along some marigolds and allamanda flowers and a few blooms from the hibiscus mutabilis bush that grew beside their hut so that she could show the children how the snow white blossoms plucked that morning slowly turned to shell-pink by noon, then darkened to rose by evening and to a dark crimson knot by nightfall. She smiled to hear them cry, 'Magic! Magic flowers!' in amazement whenever they went near the flowers she had put in a glass of water on the table: for her it was an everyday occurrence, something she could watch from her kitchen window, as common as the sweets they sucked continually and which were so rare and wonderful to her.

One evening when they sat on their veranda, for the wind was blowing hard from the sea and it was chilly, they had beside them a pot of sand into which they had stuck a branch of the casuarina tree. When Hari took their soda to them, he was puzzled to see it decked with bits of coloured paper that fluttered in the wind, and silver stars and gold balls that spun and bobbed and danced. The group on the veranda was especially gay and excited and loud that evening as grown-ups played games with children and they all sang and laughed till late at night. They ate their dinner very late and Hari reported how, while washing dishes in the kitchen, he had seen them set fire to a ball of food on a plate before eating it – he couldn't say why.

When Lila next went in to sweep, she had to clear away heaps of torn, coloured paper lying on the floor. As she carefully folded up the torn sheets and put them away in a neat heap, the mother came up and said, 'Oh, just throw them away – Christmas is over.' Puzzled, Lila carried away the paper to their hut for Bela and Kamal to see and use. 'Christmas is over,' she said and, to her surprise, the girls knew what that meant and nodded. 'Yes, Christmas. Our teacher told us about it at school. It is the birthday feast of a baby who was born long, long ago in a stable,' said Bela. 'Like Krishna, who was born in a prison,' explained Kamal when Lila looked puzzled. 'But why did they cover the tree with coloured paper and stars?' she asked, and they could not answer: their teacher had said nothing about a tree. Just then the children from the house arrived to bring them a packet of boiled sweets each, which they accepted in shy silence and later ate with noisy abandon.

'Give one to Pinto. Poor Pinto,' said Lila, feeling sorry for Pinto who had been having a very bad time for the family had brought their dog with them – a great golden creature with a plume for a tail, as beautiful as a princess in a story – and they were so afraid noisy, excited Pinto would bite their beauty whom they called Misha that they made Hari keep Pinto tied to a tree or a veranda post all day while Misha ran about in the garden, golden and gleaming and silky. At first Pinto barked and barked in fury, but when he saw it was no good, he simply lay down on the sand and sulked. He was so hurt that when Bela offered him a sweet, he turned his head away.

But soon the cloud lifted for Pinto, and one morning the car was being loaded and readied for the drive back to Bombay. Mr de Silva made Hari fetch a bucket of water and wash the car and wipe it first. As he stood watching and smoking a pipe, he said, 'Yes, that's the way. Look here, this house is falling to pieces. We need a watchman, someone to take care of it while we're away. We may not be able to come again for months and it can't be left to rot all that time. We'll pay a small salary – not much since there won't be much work, just keeping an eye on it, opening it up and airing it now and again, and letting us know if it needs repair. D'you think your father could do the job? He used to be around but I haven't seen him on this visit. Where is he?'

Hari was excited. He hurried home, knowing his father was in, lying on his mat in a dark corner. 'Father,' he said, the word rusty in his throat, he used it so seldom. 'Father, the man is calling you. He wants to give you a job.'

'Hunh? A job?' said his father, getting off the floor and coming to the door. Hari managed to guide him down the path to the house where Mr de Silva stood waiting by the car, watching it being loaded. But his expression changed when he turned towards Hari and his father. He asked a few short questions but frowned at the long, mumbled answers and turned his head away from the hot toddy breath that accompanied the mumbles. Finally he shook his head and went up the steps to the veranda to say to his wife, 'Useless, drunken villagers – dead drunk in the morning. What can you do for them? They're hopeless.'

Hari led his father back to the hut, his heart like a stone inside him, heavy and cold. Even when the de Silvas had got into the car, along with their princely dog who looked out of the window and waved his plume of a tail in excitement, and Mr de Silva leaned out of the window and gave Hari some money and said, 'Good fellow, you did a good job of the car. If you ever come to Bombay, I'll give you a job as a car-cleaner,' Hari did not, could not smile. He took the money and stood silently watching as the car bumped its way down the sandy path and disappeared into the coconut grove.

Then Lila set Pinto free at last and, giving one yelp of joy, Pinto went madly chasing the car right out of Thul.

Hari was still in a silent rage about his father's drunkenness, about the Bombay man's insulting words, when he went to see if the factory was coming up at last. He did not know if Mr de Silva would remember his promise to give him a car-cleaner's job if he ever did get to Bombay or even if he wanted it any longer. Nor did he have any idea if Biju would give him a job on his boat when it was built. So he had to see if the factory had come up and if he could get a job there: that now seemed like the best of the three choices before him.

But when he went to the site below the hill, he was disappointed to find the tin hut locked, the yellow lorry gone and only a few big concrete pipes littered on the ground to show that anyone intended to build there. When would such small beginnings ever grow into a mighty factory full of humming machines waiting to be worked by Ramu and Hari?

He walked in a circle round the pipes, almost as if he expected to see them move, but there was no movement except for a brown grasshopper that jumped out of a clump of grass on to a pipe, and then off again. So, throwing a pebble from one hand to the other and trying to whistle away his disappointment, he started walking up the hill to the temple on top, wondering what would become of it.

Steps had been cut into the red, gravelly soil of the hillside, making it easy to climb. As he brushed through the dry, golden grass that grew at the sides, he met a shepherd coming down the hill with a herd of goats. He wore a white *dhoti* and a large magenta turban and his goats were black and white and chocolate brown and followed him in a cloud of dust, bleating and calling to each other. Some of them got stranded on a spur and called frantically to the others who were already at the foot of the hill. Finally the most desperate of them bounded forward and then all the rest took heart and went streaming after him to catch up with the herd now crossing the highway to the dry fields where the winter paddy had just been cut. The shepherd's bright magenta turban could be seen as a single speck of colour in all that dust.

Hari went on up to the top with his head flung back in order to watch a pair of huge kites that seemed to be having a game in the evening sky – floating and rolling on currents of air, always close together as if they were performing a dance. He watched them as they went rolling and tumbling away in the still clear air, over the field where the girls' school stood, over the rich green belt of palms and bananas that hid his own house, and out over the sea itself, majestic and purple now with the sun dipping into it as royally as a king going to his repose. Then they vanished from sight.

When he thought of all his troubles – his drunken father, Mr de Silva's insult, the lack of work and money – Hari wished he too could soar up into the sky and disappear instead of being tied to the earth here, trudging round the temple which was not even a pretty one. It was only a little cell of bricks with a painted idol of Krishna and his cows in it. Looking at it through the open door without going in, Hari remembered the shepherd he had just seen and wondered if he, too, played a flute like Krishna. Everything belonged here, everything blended together – except for himself. With his discontent, his worries and his restlessness, he could not settle down to belonging.

He knew in his heart that he would leave one day. Thul could not hold him for long – at least not the Thul of the coconut groves and the fishing fleet. Perhaps if it really did turn into a factory site one day, he would stay on here, living a new kind of life. Otherwise he and his family would surely and slowly starve, fall ill like his mother, and die. No! He would go away – cross the sea in a boat, somehow find his fortune in Bombay, either with Mr de Silva's help or even without it. He felt very much alone.

Then he heard someone strike a match and jumped around to see a man standing behind him with a cigarette in his mouth. It was someone Hari did not know – a thin, dark man wearing a blue shirt over white pyjamas. He was staring at the idol, too.

Then he looked down at Hari. 'You from the village?' he asked, nodding in the wrong direction.

'From Thul, yes,' said Hari, pointing at the belt of coconut palms.

'Hmm,' said the stranger, 'I've met some of these Thul people.'

'Do you live here?' asked Hari, curious.

The man did not answer but pointed to the shack below.

'There?' asked Hari in amazement. 'You live in that hut? Did you come from Bombay in a lorry?'

The man nodded, smiling a little at Hari's excitement.

'Then you must be – you must be – the new factory –'

'I'm not the factory,' the man laughed. 'It's not going to be just one factory anyway – it is going to be a whole city of factories. Factories, housing colonies, shopping centres, bus depots, railway heads, engineers and workers – a whole city is going to be built here.'

'Here, in Thul?' wondered Hari, not able to believe his ears.

'Here, stretching from Thul to Vaishet, Vaishet to Rewas, and Rewas to Uran,' said the man proudly, pointing with one finger first at the coastline with its belt of coconut estates, then swivelling up the Thul road to the highway and along it to an old stone quarry that lay across the road from the hill, and then along the highway to the coastal village of Rewas. 'The new Thul-Vaishet fertilizer complex,' he said in a ringing voice.

'What is that?' asked Hari, not ashamed of showing himself an ignorant villager because he was so keen to know.

'You don't know what that is?' the man asked scornfully. 'You will learn. You will soon learn.'

'No, but tell me,' Hari said eagerly. 'What will they make at the factory?'

'Fertilizer, I told you,' the man sounded impatient.

'What is that?' Hari asked.

The man had to smile, however grimly. These villagers were such pumpkin-heads, they knew nothing. 'Chemicals,' he said, using another word that Hari did not know. 'Different kinds of chemicals to put in the ground – nitrogen, ammonia, urea – to make things grow.'

'Oh, *manure*?' asked Hari, deeply disappointed. All this vast complex, modern and scientific, to be built only to make manure for the fields?

'No, not manure, pumpkin-head. This is to stop people from following their cows and buffaloes around and collecting their dung to put in their miserable fields. Here the factories will produce tons and tons of chemicals to be sent all over the country and sold to farmers. *Rich* farmers,' he added, with another scornful look at Hari's torn shirt and bare feet, 'with *much* land. Chemicals for big farms, chemicals to make crops grow better than you can ever see them grow in fields like yours.'

'We use fish manure for our coconut trees,' Hari told him, smarting from the gibe about villagers and their buffaloes. 'It is very good for coconuts.'

'Pph! How much fish manure can you collect? Here they will make thousands of tons, tens of thousands of tons, and send it all over India and even export it.'

'Really?' said Hari politely, trying to grasp this strange new concept. 'And it will be made in many different factories?'

'Yes, of course, not one factory, but a number of factories. Industrial estate – that is what it is to be. Have you seen the one at Thana, near Bombay?'

Of course Hari had not so he shook his head and made no sound.

'This will be even bigger. What do you know?' the man seemed suddenly angry and began to walk downhill. It was steep and he had to throw himself heavily from one step to the other, his shoes slipping on the red gravel. Hari, barefoot, followed quickly and lightly, still curious, still wanting to know.

'How is fertilizer made?' he asked. 'What are the machines like? Are they worked with oil or coal? Who works them?'

'They will need people to work them,' the man shouted over his shoulder. 'A railway line will be laid. People will come from all over to work in Thul.'

'From where?' cried Hari, leaping from step to step and rock to rock, waving his arms to keep his balance.

'From everywhere,' shouted the man. 'From all over India. They will get jobs here.'

'And what about us?' Hari cried, running after him now that they had reached the foot of the hill. The stubble cut his feet.

'You?' the man wheeled around and glared at him. 'Can you work in a factory, you *boy*?'

'I can learn,' said Hari bravely, trying to keep his voice steady. 'I think I can. I need a job.'

Suddenly the man stopped glaring, or roaring. His face softened and his eyes looked kinder. 'So,' he said, 'you need a job, eh? Hungry, eh? No food in the house? Sick mother, drunken father, sisters to be married off and no dowries, eh?'

Hari was so astonished that he gave a gasp. How did this stranger know about his family? Had he been finding out about him? Why? Did he see Hari as a prospective factory-worker? Would he give Hari a job? 'How do you know?' he asked in a whisper.

The man spun around with the same expression of scorn cutting across his face. 'You villagers – you're all the same. Pumpkin-heads. Drink toddy and lie drunk under the coconut trees all day. Go fishing and drown yourself in the sea. Leave the women to manage. Old women and girls going hungry in the village. Mongrels howling in the night. Pah! What a place, your Thul. What a bunch of pumpkin-heads. All alike. I'll be happy when I can hand over charge here –' he waved at the heap of concrete pipes lying on the ground – 'and go home. To Bombay. Bombay!' he sang, lifting his arms up in the air, and then dived into his hut and slammed the door shut.

Hari stood staring at the shut door, seething with all the questions he had wanted to ask and now could not. He heard the man singing to himself, some loud and rollicking song from a Bombay film. Then the door opened, the man's face appeared in the crack, shouting, 'Pumpkin-head! Still standing there, staring? Get away, will you, leave me alone. Can't stand to see your pumpkin-face. Take it away – go – come back when you've learnt what chemicals are, what factories are, what fertilizer is good for!'

As Hari lurched homewards over the dusty ruts of the village road, a bicycle dashed past him, its bell ringing wildly. It was Ramu of course, but an unusually speedy Ramu.

'Have you heard?' he shouted back over his shoulder at Hari. 'Biju's deep freeze has arrived. A lorry brought it from Bombay.'

He sped away and did not notice that Hari shook his head: he had lost interest in old Biju the smuggler's boat. It would go out to sea and drown in the monsoon storms, the deep freeze sink to the bottom of the sea. Hari's head was filled with a vision of shining factories, tall chimneys, clouds of strange-smelling smoke, people like ants going through the big gates – and amongst them a boy in khaki shorts and a torn shirt, himself.

It was dark when he went up the path through the coconut grove. Pinto came barking towards him. He did not bother to pat him or speak to him but let him leap at his side, lovingly brushing against his legs as he walked. He could see a small fire burning in the hut, illuminating it as if it were a lamp, and the dark figures of his three sisters huddled around it, framed by the doorway.

He stepped on to the log that lay across the creek and stared at them. They could not see him in the dark and did not know he was there. Their heads were bent, they were silent, only their outlines were lit up by the flames of the small, smoking fire. They looked frightened, tired and hopeless in that huddled position in the half-dark.

Lila, Bela and Kamal. He seldom thought about them, or their lives, because they lived so close together in that small hut, sharing the same kind of life. It was the hard life that occupied him, entirely, so that he could not see them separated from it, as people, as individuals. Lila, Bela and Kamal – his three sisters, one older and two younger than him. Here they were, with nothing but a small smoking fire to light their hut or give them comfort while he was away.

What were they waiting for? What were they hoping for? They could never look forward to working on a fishing boat or in a factory, as he did. They would have to marry, one day, and he would have to see to it since his father would not. He would have to find them husbands, and buy them their wedding finery – silk saris and gold jewellery – and arrange their weddings to which the whole village would have to be invited. The bridegrooms might demand a dowry – a bicycle or even a scooter. Gold buttons, coins and jewellery. A cow or a buffalo. A piece of land. He had heard of the fantastic demands that bridegrooms made and that parents had to meet. How could he ever meet them? Even if he found a job, he would never earn enough to buy them such riches. He would have to borrow money from the village money lender and then pay him out of his salary, for years, perhaps all his life. And that was if he ever earned a salary, if he ever had a job. He must have a job if he was to find his sisters a way out of this dark, gloomy house and the illness and drunkenness and hopelessness that surrounded them like the shadows of the night.

He knew he could never earn enough in Thul to help his whole family. He would have to go to Bombay. Bombay was a great city, a rich city, a city crowded with people who had jobs, earned money and made fortunes. He had to get there somehow. How? When? That was still not clear to him.

He went into the hut, Pinto bounding ahead of him. They looked up at him. Their sad, frightened faces made him cry out, 'What has happened?'

3

I T WAS their mother. They had noticed something
strange about her ever since Lila took in her
morning tea and found she could not even lift
her head to sip it. When Lila placed an arm under
her head to raise it a bit, she felt the skin burning
and dry with fever. She called, 'Ma', and the woman
fluttered her eyelids but did not open her eyes or
smile. 'Bela, Kamal,' Lila called, and when the little
girls came running, told them to fetch cool water
from the earthen jar in the veranda and a rag to
dip in it. She placed the wet rag on her mother's
forehead and sat beside the bed, holding her
mother's wrist. It was limp between her fingers.

'What is it?' whispered the girls, bending
over the bed and staring. They were dressed and

ready for school but they would not move from the bed.

'She has fever today,' Lila murmured. 'High fever. Go tell – go and tell –'

'Who?'

'What?'

Lila bit her lip as she tried to think of an answer. After a while she spoke in a trembling voice that she tried to control. 'Go and see if you can find Hari in the field. Tell him to go to the village and ask – no, there is no doctor there.'

'Should he go to Alibagh?' Bela whispered anxiously, trying to help.

'No, that's no use – no Alibagh doctor will come all the way here,' Lila sighed. Then she said, 'Go to the Khanekars next door, Bela. Go and ask Hira-*bai* to come. Or to send a doctor. She knows doctors. She is interested in herbs and cures. Perhaps she will come herself.'

'But –' said Bela.

'What if they are all – you know?' said Kamal, with a glance at the drunken heap of her father snoring on the mat in the darkest corner of the room.

'You *have* to go. Don't talk to the men. Go straight to Hira-*bai*.'

'She drinks, too, you know,' the girls warned.

'Not all the time,' said Lila sharply. 'Go anyway, and see.'

The two girls did not argue any more but ran. As they crossed the creek by the fallen log, Pinto came dashing out of the tall grasses on the bank and met them with a delighted bark, making a heron that stood hunchbacked on a stone, staring into the marsh, give a frightened shake of its dull, grey-brown feathers, rise on its toes and flap away into the top of the pandanus grove. Other birds were startled too and called or flew out – the old hidden crow-pheasant warned 'coop-coop-coop' and a pair of drongoes swooped upwards into the sunlight, glinting blue-black. The *bhindi* tree shook down some of its yellow blossoms on to their heads.

Bela and Kamal ducked beneath its branches and scuffled through the dense shrubbery that separated their hut from their neighbour's grove. Suddenly Bela stopped, spreading out her arms to protect Kamal. Then she sighed. 'Oh it's only a skin,' and Kamal, peering over her shoulder, saw a six-foot long snake skin draped over a clump of spider lilies near Bela's foot, transparent and shimmering like a beautiful veil. It stirred in the breeze and seemed almost alive. Its mouth was open, and there were even two little holes for the eyes – it was so perfect and whole. But it was only a dry skin, probably discarded the night before, so the girls held hands and hurried past it to the Khanekars' estate.

The Khanekars lived in a large, sprawling untidy house in the midst of all that vegetation, the weeds crawling closer to their mud walls and the vines climbing over the thatch roof. The yard was littered with heaps of firewood, empty clam shells, a few clucking hens and some shabby grey laundry spread out to dry over the bushes. It was all neglected and shabby. At one time they had groves of betel leaf, banana plantations, poultry and a tank in which they kept freshwater fish. But the three brothers who owned the land did not care for agriculture or fishing and after their father died, they stopped working altogether and drank the toddy they brewed themselves and sold what was left to other drunkards. Their wives had left them and gone back to their parents in other villages. Only their old mother, Hira-*bai*, kept house for them. She was fond of toddy, too.

However, to the relief of the little girls, she was sitting cross-legged on a string bed outside her house, competently chopping up a heap of betel nuts into small slivers that she dropped into a large metal box at her side. Her mouth was stained a deep red from the betel leaves and betel nuts that she chewed all day. She opened that crimson mouth in a surprised grin when she saw them and automatically adjusted the fold of her purple sari over her grey head as women always did when visitors appeared.

'Ho, Bela. Ho, Kamal. What brings you here? Your father sent you for a pot of toddy this early in the morning?' she shouted, and burst into loud laughter which made a man, invisible in the house, call out, 'What's up, Mother?'

Bela and Kamal stopped short at some distance from her. Kamal twisted one leg about the other and put her finger in her mouth. Bela did the same.

Hira-*bai* cackled with laughter. 'Don't like to say, eh? Don't like to ask for toddy? Don't be shy. We know what men are like. You know, and I know, so why be shy?'

The girls shook their heads at her, speechlessly.

'Eh? No toddy, you say? Then what's it you want? Money for toddy?'

More vigorously, they shook their heads till their plaits flew.

'Not money for toddy? Well – your ma sent you then? For money for rice? For tea? Is that it? No rice in the house? Now girls, before you ask for any, I'd better warn you –'

Suddenly Bela could bear it no longer. Breaking away from Kamal, she came a few steps closer and said quickly in a hoarse voice, 'We don't want money. We don't want rice. We haven't come to ask for any. My mother is sick and my sister sent us to tell you to please –'

'Sick?' the old woman stared at Bela and stopped laughing. 'I know she is sick. She is always sick. Is she worse then?'

Bela nodded rapidly. 'She has fever. We have no medicine. Can you call a doctor to see her?'

The old woman began cutting betel nuts again with her powerful scissors. She mumbled to herself as she did so. Then she stopped chop-chopping the hard little wooden nuts and spoke in a different voice. 'I'll tell you what. I heard the old man who comes to the village with his cow blowing his horn and banging his drum early this morning. He can't have gone far. I'll send word to him to turn around and come back. I'll send him to you. He has good herbs, powders and barks. Go and tell Lila,' she said, nodding to them encouragingly so that her sari slipped off her head and showed the grey hair dyed bright orange with henna.

Bela and Kamal turned and fled, fighting their way through the shrubbery back to the safety of their home. But before they came to the log across the creek they heard a yelp and turned to see Pinto, who had stayed back to sniff at the chickens in the coop and the fish bones in a heap by the house, come limping and squealing after them, his tail between his legs and his ears flattened. Either the old woman or one of the men in the house must have flung a stone or a coconut at him and hit him in the leg. He came up to them whining and they hurried him home before any more stones could be flung.

At the hut there was nothing to do but wait. Lila did not say anything about school as she went about her housework in a silent, tight-lipped way, now and then going to see to their mother, and the girls stayed outside the hut, playing in a quiet, subdued way, drawing patterns in the sand and decorating the patterns with flower petals. Now and then Lila gave them some task to do and these they did at once, without arguing. They fetched water from the well, washed the pot in which the tea had been made, cleaned the rice for their lunch and then searched around the shrubbery for firewood.

At last they heard the throbbing of the drum and the long eerie blasts on the trumpet which meant the medicine-man was near. He was preceded by the little dwarf cow that he dressed in tassels and necklaces of beads, with an embroidered cloth covering her hump. They had often seen him take the rounds with her, offering bundles of grass to people who would buy the bundle and feed it to the cow. Feeding the cow was a pious act and they were glad to pay a little and perform it. It brought him some money but not enough so he combined this occupation of ushering the sacred cow around the villages with the selling and administering of medicines that he found in the forest and prepared himself. He was a sharp-looking man and he kept all kinds of powders and pills in packets tied into the folds of his white *dhoti* and his pink turban. With these he treated the villagers for their boils, aches and fevers. He was also known to perform special *puja* for those who were too ill to benefit from his powders – the mad, the unhappy and the dying. All this gave him the air of a magician, of witchcraft, which made the girls shiver slightly when they heard him approach.

He raised his hand in the air as he marched over the log on the creek and gave another long blast on his trumpet which was made of bone. The bone of what? the girls wondered uneasily.

Lila came running out of the house and Bela and Kamal clung to Pinto to prevent him from attacking the holy cow. They would have liked to go closer and inspect the dwarf creature but Lila wanted them to keep Pinto away while she spoke to the man.

'My mother is ill. She has been ill for a long time. Now she has fever too. Have you any medicine for fever? Have you any medicine for making her strong? She is so weak,' Lila explained.

'Slowly, slowly, daughter. What is the hurry? First I must have water for my cow – fresh well water. Next, I must have grass for her. Fresh, tender grass. Then I will come and see your mother.'

So that was how things had to be done. After the cow had been looked after, he too demanded attention. Lila had to heat a tumbler of tea for him which he sipped, sitting on a string cot under the frangipani tree while the girls stood before him and told him how their mother was growing weaker and weaker, refusing to eat and unable to get up at all. 'And now she is hot with fever,' Lila wailed suddenly, no longer able to speak calmly.

The man looked at her with his sharp, bright eyes, understanding how it was with her. He got up quickly and started being very busy. To their surprise he did not go in to see to their mother as they had expected he would. Instead, he ordered them to build a fire on the threshold of the hut. He watched them critically and ordered them about: he wanted a particular kind of wood and the sticks had to be laid just so. Once it had started crackling and smoking, he flung in packets of flowers that he took from a bag slung on to the cow's back – jasmine and marigold, hibiscus and frangipani. He recited a long prayer in Sanskrit in a sing-song undertone while he did so, and the fire crackled and spat. The three girls sat on their heels around the fire, their chins resting on their hands, watching. When the fire had died down, he poked at it with a long stick, scattering the ashes so that they cooled. Then he scooped them up into his cupped hand and asked for water.

They brought him a tumbler and he poured a little into the palm of his hand and with one thumb and forefinger he mixed it with the ash. Then he went in to see their mother at last.

She was lying on her side with her eyes closed. When he spoke to her, she turned over and opened her eyes in fear. Lila put her hand on her forehead and spoke to her soothingly. The man told her to open her mouth and put out her tongue which she did, and on it he dropped some of the ash. 'Eat, sister,' he said. 'Holy ash, purified ash. It will purify you within. It will drive away the demons that create the fever. Swallow.' He kept rolling small balls of ash between his fingers and dropping them into her mouth, making her swallow them. Then he clapped his hands together, broke into the loud recitation of prayers, and walked out.

The girls followed, dazed.

'Sweep up all that ash. Collect it. Bring it to me,' he ordered, and they obeyed. He pulled some leaves out of his bag and made them put the ash on the leaves, then rolled them up and tied them into neat packets with bits of thread that he pulled out of his turban. 'Here,' he said, handing them to the girls. 'Go and put one packet under her pillow. It will drive away the fever-demon. Go and put the others under your own pillows. It will keep you safe from the demons. I have blessed it. Hari Om, Hari Om, Hari Om,' he bellowed suddenly and, lifting his trumpet, blew a long blast on it that made Pinto, tied to a post, howl furiously.

Lowering the trumpet, he stared down into their faces and looked very fierce. They noticed that his moustache bristled like a brush and that it was stained with tobacco. 'So?' he shouted at them. 'What do you do now? Stare at my face? Got nothing to give me but your stares? Think I can fill my stomach with that? Think I do it all for free?'

Lila shook herself guiltily and ran into the hut, Bela and Kamal staring after her in agony, knowing there was no money. But she came out with something in her hand and when she handed it over the girls saw what it was – the ring their mother used to wear when she was well and that she had taken off and kept behind the mirror on the shelf now that she was ill. It was of silver – rather blackened and twisted now, but still silver. The girls gave a little gasp of astonishment but the man merely snatched it out of Lila's hand, stared at it, then at them, tucked it away into one of his pouches and marched off towards his cow without a word of thanks.

He set off with her, alternately stroking the hide-drum to draw long, strange sounds out of it, blowing on his trumpet and calling, 'Hari Om, Hari Om,' into the sky. Birds flew up in fright, screaming and wheeling till he was out of sight and hearing.

The girls were left staring at the leaf-packets in their hands.

'What shall we do with them?' Bela and Kamal asked.

Lila clutched the one in her hand as if she wanted to tear it apart or throw it away. 'What shall we do?' she cried. 'We can't do anything – we have to listen to him. There's no hospital in the village we could take her to, and no doctor who would come. We have no one but the magic man to help us. Magic!' she said fiercely and turned and marched into the hut to do what the man had told her to.

The girls were frightened enough by these events but the day seemed to be a cursed one and had still more shocks and alarms in store for them.

As they lay stretched on mats on the cool clay floor of the hut in the afternoon, dozing, they were woken first by Pinto's sudden bark and then the barks of a great many other dogs near by. Kamal got up at once, trying to hush Pinto but the noise the dogs made outside grew louder and louder. Pinto was so frantic that she could not hold him back, he pulled away from her and darted out. She followed and stood under the tattered palm thatch of the veranda, staring into the white-hot glare of the afternoon.

A band of men, boys and mongrels had invaded the dense shrubbery that surrounded the creek. All the quiet birds that haunted it – the moorhen, the heron, the kingfishers and egrets – had flown. The men were trampling down the pandanus, breaking the slim stems of the casuarinas and beating the rushes and grasses with the long sticks they carried, howling and yelling as if they were cavemen hunting in ancient times. The mongrels that usually lay about on the beach, half asleep, now yapped and yowled with excitement. For once they were not beaten with sticks or driven away – they were being used in the hunt.

'What are they doing?' whispered Bela who had crept out to stand beside her sister and watch, frightenedly.

'I don't know,' Kamal whispered back. 'The way they are screaming, it seems there is an elephant there, or a man-eater. Perhaps it is a cobra.'

Bela gave a shudder, feeling an icy finger run down her spine.

'Look at Pinto!' she suddenly cried. 'Pinto's going with them – catch him.'

That made Kamal run down the path after the dog – she did not want a stick or stone hurled at him, nor the fiercely yapping and snarling dogs to attack him who was not of their pack.

As she caught up with Pinto on the bank of the creek, now trampled and turned to green, oozing mud by all the stamping feet and paws, the band of hunters pressed on and surrounded a grove of pandanus. Here they fell upon their prey with a great hullabaloo, bringing down their sticks with great whacks while the dogs leapt and darted about in frenzy.

In spite of her fear and horror of the scene, Kamal could not help being curious and asked an old man who stood at the outer edge of the ring, grinning and scratching one leg with the other, 'What is it? What have they caught?'

'See, see.' The old man grinned, pointing delightedly to where the creature was being torn apart by the dogs, then torn out of their mouths by the men who heaved it up on top of a pole, like a trophy.

'Oh,' cried Kamal in distress, clasping her hands together and nearly crying. 'It's only a little mongoose.'

The old man rolled his yellow eyes at her. 'It is bad – very bad,' he told her. 'It drinks the water out of our coconuts. When they are green and fresh, it climbs the trees, makes a small hole in the coconut and drinks all the sweet juice so that the nuts falls down – dry.' He slapped his hand on his thigh and went off chuckling to join the celebration over the capture and death.

Kamal stood stricken on the mound by the creek, holding Pinto by the neck. A poor, small, helpless mongoose – she did not believe it did anything so wicked; it was a mistake. And even if it did drink the coconut water and destroy the coconuts, was it necessary to hunt it with a dozen sticks, a pack of wild dogs and a band of howling men? It frightened her to see the ferocity with which they had destroyed the little thing.

When she heard Bela coming down the path to join her and stare at the men and dogs who went whooping down the blazing white beach to celebrate, she turned to go back to the house. 'Come, Pinto, come,' she begged the dog, in tears.

Later that evening, with Hari still not back, their father already out, leaving the girls to sit around their mother's door, wondering why her fever had not come down, another visitor broke through the thick, wild hedge, sending the bright red, hard wooden fruit of the pandanus rolling with a kick of his foot.

This time it was Lila who got to her feet, pushing the two girls behind her when she saw it was one of the three drunken brothers who lived in the neighbouring grove. From his rolling walk, his wildly disordered hair and red eyeballs, it was easy to see he was already drunk although the sky still held the evening light, the sea was bronze and calm, and it was by no means the hour at which most men in the village started to drink. But of course he brewed his own toddy and must have been lying in his house drinking all day, Lila knew. She was frightened.

'Oh you, you child of a rascal,' he roared at her, standing by the log across the creek and swaying on his feet. 'Where's that father of yours, that rascal?'

'My father?' said Lila wildly. 'He – he has gone out.'

'Gone out – or hiding under his wife's bed? Shall I come and drag him out?'

Lila gave a small scream which was echoed by the two girls who were hiding behind her. Now Pinto was growling, too, although held back by them from attacking the intruder. 'He's not here,' she cried in a high-pitched voice. 'Don't come in – my mother is ill.'

'Oh very good, very good.' He laughed maliciously, showing his yellow teeth in a mouth stained red with betel juice. 'Mother ill – father out – little girls know nothing. Do you at least know where he keeps his money?' he roared suddenly, like a lion, making Lila shrink back.

'Money?' she murmured, clenching her fists and wishing Hari would appear. 'We have no money.'

'No money – we have no money,' he mocked her. 'Very nice answer. Did he teach you to tell me that – that rogue, your father? Like father, like daughter. A family of liars, no-goods. No money, no good – all of you. But wait till I catch him. I'll break his neck and find the money all right.'

Pinto, giving an uncontrollable yelp of rage at this man who stood shouting and swaying and waving his arms about in front of their house, suddenly broke away from the girls, darted past Lila and was out on the path, digging up sand with agitated claws, showing his sharp teeth and barking like a proper guard dog. He approached the man in short leaps and bounds, and when he was close enough to bite, the man raised his arms and roared, 'Call that dog back. If you don't keep him off – I'll kill him.'

Bela and Kamal, screaming together, darted out after Pinto, flying to save him from the drunkard. Seeing them all out on the path, ready for a battle, Lila hurried after them, calling, 'Pinto – Pinto – come back. Bela, Kamal, catch him. He won't bite – he won't bite –'

'If he bites,' the man roared, 'I'll – I'll –'

The uproar brought them some help after all. It was his old mother, the woman who had sent them the magic-man that morning, who came hobbling through the gap in the hedge to see what it was all about. Seeing her son there, tottering drunkenly in a circle and shouting, she grabbed him by the arm and gave him a quick, sharp shake.

'*You*,' she said fiercely, 'you *idiot*. What are you doing here, frightening these little girls? Get back to the house – do you hear? Get back – you're not fit to go out or talk to anyone. Go, hide yourself in your dirty black mud-hole. Stick your head in your toddy-pot and don't show it around here again. Go.' She gave him a push and he, silent now, stumbled off, half falling over the round pandanus fruit and muttering to himself, 'Go, go, go, they say. Where shall I go? I want my money. I'll get my money. I'll kill that rogue. I'll kill his dog –'

'Be quiet,' his mother screamed after him, picking up a stick and hitting it hard against a tree trunk. 'Be quiet, I say,' she screamed again and went off after him without another look at the girls who stood like shadows cast by the coconut palms on the sand.

Then they turned and filed back to the house silently. Lila lit the fire early, to drive away the shadows that seemed so threatening, so full of danger tonight. They were sitting around that small fire when Hari came home to ask, 'What has happened?' and they could burst out at last and tell him. There was nothing he could do – they knew that – to make their mother well, to keep away the drunken neighbour or his threats, to save Pinto from him and save them all from the cruelty all around them, but it helped that he, too, knew their fears and shared their troubles.

4

HARI knew now that he could not continue to sit in the silent shadowy hut with his sisters, nor trail along the beach with his empty net, nor go lurking around the shack at the foot of the hill with the temple in the hope of a job that might not come through for years. He had to act, since there was no one else in the family fit to act and action was needed.

Next morning he went stumbling over the baking white sand of the beach to join the group around Biju's boat which was now beginning to look nearly ready. With the deep freeze installed in it, Biju would not leave the boat night or day. It was said he slept on the deck as if the boat were already at sea. Now, in the bright morning light, he sat – seemed to be planted – on the folding chair, his palms pressed against his knees, watching as the men crawled about the boat, polishing and painting and planing. A sheet of tin, painted bright blue with the figure of a pink and white mermaid in the centre, was tacked above the cabin door. A man was carefully writing the boat's name below the mermaid: *Jal Pari*, mermaid. Hoots of laughter went up from the village boys hanging around when it became clear what the name was, and Biju turned on them with a fierce look.

Hari stopped to see why they were laughing. They pointed at the pink and white mermaid frolicking in the bright blue sea and made rude jokes about her. 'Biju's building the boat so he can go and catch her,' they said, and winked. But Hari did not feel like smiling. He left them and walked slowly but straight up to old Biju himself. In the night he had resolved to ask Biju for a job on the boat.

But Biju turned his head away for just at that moment someone else was approaching him, a stranger who had to be attended to first. Hari saw it was the man from the tin shack, the watchman who guarded the pipes, the beginnings of the great factory.

'So, yet another fishing boat ready to catch fish for the people of Thul?' called the man jovially, walking up to Biju with a cheap leaf-cigarette in his mouth, unlit.

Biju's face darkened, and he frowned. 'This is no ordinary fishing boat,' he growled. 'Can't you see that with your own eyes? It has a diesel engine, it has a deep freeze, it has the capacity to travel fifty miles a day.'

'Oh ho,' laughed the stranger, striking a match to his leaf-cigarette and puffing at it as he stared at the boat.

Just then the tin signboard flew off the nail and on to the deck with a clatter. It had to be picked up and hung again, the paint smeared and dripping. The boys cackled and old Biju growled ferociously at the painter who started dabbing at it with a rag and nervously repairing the damage.

'So, a mighty sea trawler is being built here, is it?' said the stranger sarcastically. 'Fifty miles it will go? Well, it will have to – if it is to catch any fish.'

'What do you mean? There is plenty of fish around here,' Biju growled at him, shifting uncomfortably on the folding chair.

'No, there is not,' said the stranger, lowering himself on to his heels and squatting comfortably on the sand. 'There is hardly any fish left here. Yesterday I wanted to buy a pomfret for my dinner and got only one small miserable one. No one in Bombay would eat a pomfret of that size,' he said scornfully, making the villagers fall silent and listen. 'And if you ask for prawns, all you get are miserable little shrimps. Not enough for Bombay people – not enough for even you villagers. It's time you gave up your boats and nets and turned to something new.'

'We have always fished in the sea here,' said Biju stoutly, making Hari and the other boys feel a certain pride in him, their richest and biggest fisherman. 'Always will. And if there is not enough fish for us, there is plenty of food anyway – paddy and vegetables and coconuts. Where else in this country do you get such good crops? The coconuts are so big and sweet, they sell for good money in Bombay. The land is so good, we grow two crops in a year. We have the best paddy. Have you eaten our good rice?'

'Yes, yes,' said the man, spitting out bits of tobacco. 'I've had your rice. I've seen your fields. They will soon go. All the land will be bought up, factories will be built on it. Your rice will go.'

The boys looked at each other and nodded, bright-eyed. This was what they had been telling the elders in the village, only they had not been believed. Now they were hearing it from the man concerned, they would have to believe. They quite enjoyed the look of horror and agitation on old Biju's dark, frowning face.

'No one can take our land,' said Biju who owned three acres of paddy and two of coconut and betel palms, apart from his fishing fleet. 'It is ours, and we will not sell.'

'When the government says sell, you will sell all right,' said the stranger, snapping his fingers, 'like that. No questions asked. You will have to – the government has chosen this place as the right one for its factories and factories will be built.'

'Why here?' Biju challenged him. 'Go build your factories where the land is barren and nothing grows but stones and thorns.' He waved in the direction of the Kankeshwar hills that separated the green belt along the coast from the barren hinterland. 'Why should we sell our good farmland for factories?'

'You will have to sell – it is the place the government has chosen.'

'How can the government choose without asking us?'

'Who will ask you, old man?' said the stranger. 'They sent their experts to find the right kind of land – and this is what they chose. It is near the port of Rewas so it will have transport to Bombay. It is close to Bombay – only fourteen kilometres away. They can lay a railway line here easily. The road already exists and only needs to be widened. Transport is good. It is near the sea and the wastes can be pumped into it. There is enough land for the factories, the housing colonies, all the people who will come here to work.'

'People? What people are to come and work here?'

'Thousands,' laughed the man. 'Thousands will come. Whole colonies will have to be built for them, buses and trains laid on for them, and markets –'

'And what about us who already live here?' asked Biju angrily, his face quite purple.

The stranger laughed and chopped at the air with his hand as if he were cutting down weeds. 'Like that – your village will go. In its place, factories will come up, fertilizer will be made, gas will be produced, many jobs will be created.

The government says so,' he added loudly when he became aware of the angry looks of the villagers.

'Fishermen and farmers are now to become factory workers?' shouted Biju. 'You mean these boys are to give up their fathers' lands and boats and go to work in factories like city people?'

'These boys?' The man turned his head and gave them a cool look where they stood listening intently. 'I don't know about these boys – I only know about the engineers and mechanics who will have to be brought from elsewhere to run the factories.'

'And us?' shouted Ramu suddenly, instead of Hari who only felt a dry tickling in his throat, making him want to speak and preventing him from doing so.

'You?' the man looked at him scornfully. 'This old man can put you in his boat and send you off to catch fish – fifty miles away.' He laughed. 'Far, far away,' he roared, waving his hand out to the sea that glittered and swelled under the white sun.

The village was filled with anger. Hari could sense it everywhere as he walked up the village lane to the temple. He had promised Lila he would see if there was any ice for sale and bring some for their mother who was hot with fever. Although the scene was as quiet as usual – bright saris hanging up to dry on veranda rails, women watering the sacred basil plants by their doors, market women arranging and rearranging their flower garlands and bananas on leaves spread before them – there was something in the air, the languid lazy atmosphere replaced by one of stiffness, resentment, anger.

Feeling it so distinctly and strongly, Hari was not surprised to see that a large group of people had collected outside the brick hall of the temple. Not only idle young boys and fishermen with nothing else to do, but also the farmers who owned the big coconut and betelnut estates, and even women and girls – all stood in a close cluster, listening to a young man who stood on the top step of the stairs that led up to the temple. He was giving a speech and Hari drew closer to listen to him.

'I have come from Alibagh to ask you to join us. We are all concerned in this matter – all of us who live here in these fourteen villages along the coast from Rewas to Alibagh. Every one of us is threatened. Our land is going to be taken away. Where we grow coconuts and good rice for our families, they want to build their factories. Our crops will be destroyed so that their factories can come up instead. All the filth of their factories – for when you produce fertilizers, a lot of effluents are created which have to be disposed of – these will be dumped in the sea and will kill the fish for miles around. How will we live without our land, without the sea?' he called over their heads in a ringing voice, flinging out his arms to include them in the dilemma.

'How will we live?' they called back in one voice. Hari heard himself shout, 'How?' and was surprised by the sound.

'They will send their men to pacify you – to pacify you with lies. The men will tell you that you will get jobs. I tell you that they cannot give us all jobs. The factories will be run by trained engineers, by men with degrees from colleges in the city. There may be a few jobs for simple people like us who have never gone to school but have spent our lives in producing food for other people. Jobs as sweepers, jobs as coolies – the worst jobs, the most ill-paid jobs. Yes, they will let us have those. But it is the engineers who will be paid well, who will be given houses to live in – engineers from the city. They say they only need five hundred acres for their factories, but thousands more will be needed for the housing colonies, and for all the small factories that always come up around the big ones. They will take at least two thousand five hundred acres from us of our best land – the richest land in Maharashtra. In return they will cut down our tall green coconut trees, destroy our paddy crops, kill the fish in the sea, and then we will be driven away because we will be no use to them. Can we let this happen to us?' he roared.

'No, no, no,' the people roared back. 'We will not! We will not!'

'Then come with us to Bombay to tell the Chief Minister Sahib what we think of his plans. We have already spoken to the District Commissioner at Alibagh, and he has done nothing for us. A Minister Sahib is said to have come and spoken to us. The truth is, when he saw us waiting for him, he took fright and got into his car and sped back to Bombay, leaving the police to deal with us. The police drove us away with their batons.

We will not stand for this treatment. We will not stand for police rule!' he roared, his long hair flying about his shoulders and his arms raised to the sky.

'No police rule! No police rule!' chanted the audience, Hari amongst them, pounding the back of the boy who stood in front of him as he called out the words lustily.

'Now we must go direct to the Chief Minister. If he won't come and listen to us, we will go and make him listen where he sits in his office in Bombay,' roared the young man. 'Who will come with me? Will you come?'

'Yes, yes, yes!' roared the crowd, even the women and children who had never been further than Alibagh and had neither the bus nor the ferry fare in their pockets.

'Then meet me at Rewas, at the pier, tomorrow morning at daybreak, and we will set out in the fishing boats. We will sail to Bombay. We will meet the Minister Sahib in his office and make him listen to us. They will be frightened when they see us come, they will have to sit quietly and listen. We will tell them they can't take our land, they can't take the sea from us – the land is ours, the sea is ours!'

'Ours! Ours! Ours!' called the people, all raising their arms into the air and waving them like so many palms on the land, so many sails on the sea.

When Hari finally reached the shop that sometimes had a consignment of ice from the ice factory in Alibagh to sell to the fishermen, he was told it had not arrived yet, there was a delay, traffic was being held up on the highway by a massive procession of farmers and fishermen agitating against the fertilizer factory.

Hari nodded. He knew all about that. But he needed the ice. He had nothing else to do with his day, so he sat down in the dust by a hibiscus bush near the shop to wait for the ice. He was glad of the shade and the quiet around the empty shop. He needed to be alone and to think things over by himself.

Since he had left his home in the morning – and indeed earlier than that, since last night when his sisters had seemed to be asking something of him without actually speaking – he had felt buffeted by the crowds, shoved now in this direction and now in that, and did not know which way he should choose.

Down on the beach earlier that morning, he had been prevented from asking Biju for a job by the dialogue between the city man and Biju. Listening to it, he had felt that the sarcastic, knowing watchman from the city was cleverer, shrewder and more in the right than old, bad-tempered Biju and all those clownish workmen on the boat and the idle boys who dropped out of school and had nothing to do but stand around and joke and laugh. He had given up the idea of asking Biju for work and felt like crossing over to the city man's side, not to the side of the idle, lazy, clumsy village boys. He could see the sense and reason in the man's words although his way of speaking had hurt him and made him turn against him as the older villagers did.

Then, listening to the forceful speech of the young man from Alibagh – someone told him his name was Adarkar and that he was a member of the Maharashtra State Legislative Assembly whom they themselves had elected in the last elections – he had felt he must stand beside his fellow villagers and fight for the right of the farmers and fishermen to earn their living by the traditional ways, even if he had neither land nor boat to fight for.

What should he do? Should he join the villagers and march to Bombay and take part in the protest against this taking over of their land and occupations? Or should he take the part of the government and the factory and try to find work there in the new, strange manner brought to them from the distant city? As he turned over these questions in his mind, he found it was the idea of going to Bombay that excited him most. That was partly because he was attracted to the thought of fighting for his land along with the other villagers and partly because of the thought of going to Bombay at last. Here was the chance to go that he had been waiting for all along. Did he dare to take it – a young, penniless boy who had never been anywhere?

He sat in the shade with his head bowed, drawing lines in the dust with a twig, till at last the lorry arrived with a block of ice wrapped in a gunny sack along with some other provisions – kerosene, sugar, molasses and wheat. Hari got up hastily to stand close to the block of ice while the shopkeeper chipped at it so as to make it fit into his ice box. He collected the chips in a piece of cloth he had with him, then bought a small piece for money so as not to anger the shopkeeper, and hurried back down the beach to get it home before it melted. He felt a certain happiness in having something to take to his mother and to Lila which dispelled his worries for a little while.

As soon as he came up the path by the creek, he realized there was something wrong. He heard the wails of his sisters, loud and clear in the still house, and broke into a run, thinking it was his mother, his mother who had –

'Lila!' he shouted. 'Lila! What's happened?'

She was standing at the doorpost, leaning her head against it, and crying, not loudly like her sisters, but quietly and heartbrokenly. He rushed up to catch her by the arm and shout, 'Mother? Is it Mother? Here, I've got the ice for her – here's the ice –'

She shook her head and, shutting her eyes, pointed to a corner of the hut. He went in, his knees shaking, to see, and found it was Pinto she pointed at – Pinto stretched out on the ground, stiff like a piece of board found on the beach, his hair matted, his eyes open and sightless. He went and knelt by the dog, staring but not daring to touch.

Then Bela and Kamal came and flung themselves at him, burrowing their weeping faces into his shoulder and pulling at his arm.

'What happened?' he asked in a whisper. 'He was quite all right this morning.'

Lila had come to stand behind them, crying. 'He has been poisoned,' she wept. 'He suddenly fell ill – started vomiting here in front of the house – blood – there was blood in the vomit – and then he fell down and died. It is poison, I know – I know,' she wailed, both in sorrow and in fear.

'Who would poison Pinto?' Hari asked, bewildered, flinging down the piece of ice in order to touch the dog's wet, matted fur and try to feel some breath, some life left in the body.

'I know who it was,' shrieked Kamal. 'It was that – that horrible old man – that drunkard who lives over there,' she shouted, pointing at their neighbour's land.

'Yes, it was he who threatened us,' said Lila sadly. 'He did say he would punish us – that he would kill Pinto.'

'Why?' shouted Hari, in a rage, beginning to cry a little bit himself. 'Why should he kill our Pinto?'

'He hates us,' Bela and Kamal wailed.

'He said he would punish us,' Lila remembered, 'because Father had not paid him for some toddy. He said Father owed him some money, Father was in debt.'

'Debt, debt, debt,' Hari gnashed his teeth. 'Father's always in debt because of toddy.' He got up and turned away from the dead dog and his wailing sisters, and walked out of the house. He would get away. He would go to Rewas. To Bombay. And never come back to this sad house, his frightened sisters, his ill mother, his drunken father. He would leave them and run, run as far away as he could go.

5

HE DID not know that next morning Biju's boat was to be launched as the tide came up with the sun. Villagers came pouring out of their huts hidden in the greenery on to the shining white beach to watch. Biju's wife had hoisted a whole cluster of flags and banners on the deck – old saris of hers cut and stitched into long banners, pink and green and violet, and flags that were a patchwork of several saris, patterned and flowered and checked in saffrons, maroons and blues. The newly painted signboard was up on the cabin wall, bright blue and pink. Biju sat resplendent on his folding chair, his arms folded across his chest which swelled with pride.

Last evening the boatbuilders had sunk two winches in the sand, attached by strong ropes to the boat. Now, in the morning, palm tree trunks were laid across the sand from the boat to the edge of the sea. A man carrying a tin full of black oil was painting the trunks with it to make the boat slide easily. Biju's wife and daughter stood ready with trays of sweets to pass around as the boat flew down into the sea. Now the wife stepped forward to break a coconut open on its prow where a pair of eyes had been painted, black and white. The coconut cracked and spattered to shouts and cheers from all.

Now the boat was heaved up and lifted on to the oiled tree trunks. The bamboo poles that stuck out of the winches like so many arms were seized by the sweating, muscular workmen who began to wrap them round and round, unwinding the ropes with such enthusiasm that the boat, which was not held back with any other ropes, lurched wildly across the greased logs and tilted dangerously, listing to one side and making everyone abandon ropes and run for their lives. There it tilted, drunkenly, nearly toppling on to its side and falling on the sand.

The happy beam was wiped off old Biju's face and a cloud as black as thunder crossed it. He got off his folding chair and came waddling down to see what had happened. His wife and daughter stood clutching their trays of sweets in silent dismay. The young boys who had gathered to stare all hooted and laughed. The boatbuilders stood about, grinning foolishly. No one knew what to do next.

Biju cursed the workers, lashing them with abuse. 'Should have brought my men from Alibagh to do it – you pumpkins from the fields, what do you know about boats?'

'Where are they today, your men from Alibagh?' asked a man with casually folded arms.

'They've all gone to Rewas today, to catch the boat to Bombay,' answered one of the young boys, laughing. 'They're going to try and stop the government from building the fertilizer factory here. They want to go on being farmers and fishermen and fools all their lives,' he hooted, waving at the confused scene around the hopelessly toppled boat. 'All our lives we're supposed to go on building tubs like this one here, and go to sea in them to drown.'

'Oh, is that so?' Biju turned upon him. 'You don't know how to build boats, how to fish, how to sail – you know nothing – you young jackass. What you need is a good thrashing.'

'We know better than that, old Biju,' answered the young boy coolly – it was Hari's friend, Ramu. 'We will get jobs in the factory. We will have good, safe jobs and money in our pockets while you go out fighting the sea to catch a few stinking fish. Then we'll see who knows better, you or we.' All the boys who stood around him, listening admiringly to his speech, began to laugh at the old man and his boat, calling it 'pumpkin-shell' and 'empty coconut' till he raised his heavy-muscled arms in the air and roared at them, 'Get out, get away from here before I get my stick and lay it across your backs.'

They turned away laughing and one of them asked, 'Where's Hari? He hasn't come to watch the fun.'

'Dunno,' replied Ramu. 'D'you think he's gone to Rewas with the men from Alibagh?'

'He'd be a fool if he has,' said another.

They drifted off, kicking up sand as they went. Some stayed back and stood about while the workmen tried to pull the ropes and right the boat, then gave up. 'Let's wait till the tide comes up,' they said, wiping the sweat from their faces. 'The tide will set the boat right and it'll launch itself,' they explained to Biju and also drifted away, saying they were tired and wanted tea.

Only Biju, his wife and daughter, all in their new clothes, were left on the beach, helpless. After a while the heat of the sun drove them away too.

The tide did not come up high enough to lift the boat. Next day the men tried again to upright it and launch it, but so dispiritedly, so without will or enthusiasm, that they failed. They had to try again and again, for many days – angry with Biju for forcing them to do it, and Biju angry with them for failing – and finally they inched it down the beach to the tide line where it was put to sea quietly and ignominiously in the dark of the night.

By then Hari was so far away from Thul, he had forgotten all about the boat *Jal Pari*.

6

WHEN Hari reached Rewas, dawn was breaking and the people who had gathered there in the night were getting down into the small fishing boats that bobbed up and down beside the pier.

Hari climbed down from the bullock cart in which he had spent the night and looked in his pocket for some coins to give the driver but the man waved his whip in the air and said, 'Go, run. There are the boats you wanted to catch. Mine will come in later, I'll go and have a glass of tea in the meantime. Don't pay me – I did nothing for you, I was coming here anyway.' Then he brought his whip down on his bullock's back, making it heave the cart forwards and go rumbling towards a wayside teashop.

Hari felt stiff from his night on the bare boards of the bullock cart. He had hoped to catch a bus to Rewas and had spent an hour standing on the highway by Thul, alone in the dark, before he realized that the last bus to Rewas must have gone. So he hailed a bullock cart and asked for a lift which he was given.

'Come, get in – I have to reach Rewas before daybreak. I am to meet a man who is bringing goods from Bombay for our village; he has ordered me to meet him. Food for his fields, he says – fertilizer. You know what that is?'

Hari was astonished to hear that unlikely word in the middle of the night on a bullock cart, but he felt he did not know enough to be able to explain so he climbed in silently. It was completely bare, not even a sack on the creaking, sliding boards. As the bullock cart lurched forwards, he too lurched forwards, then backwards and, as the cart began to rumble on, he was pitched from side to side, getting rubbed and sore from the uneven boards which were not even smooth but splintered and full of knobs and knots. He sat clutching the sides and trying to keep himself from sliding about by pushing his feet against the ledge. 'Fertilizer is a kind of manure, I think,' he told the driver. 'Like cowdung and compost. But different. You have to buy it.'

'That's right. Now we want everything to come from the shops, ready-made. No more spinning of yarn, no more grinding of wheat at home – and no more making of cowdung cakes or compost. I don't know why. What is this new disease? Expensive, that's what it is,' complained the driver, more to hear himself speak in the night than out of any strong feeling. His voice was mild, and sleepy.

'Perhaps it is not enough any more,' Hari called back over his shoulder.

'Not enough, not enough,' agreed the cart driver. 'Nothing is enough. We are too many on earth now. Not enough fuel for all, not enough food, not enough jobs – or schools, or hospitals, or trains, buses or houses. Too many people, not enough to go around. It was not so,' he sighed and, hunching his shoulders, he let his chin sink on to his chest, closed his eyes and let the bullock carry him on down the straight road through the fields.

For a while Hari sat watching the white dusty road as it seemed to flow from under the cart like a moonlit river, and at the fields on either side, bare now that the winter wheat crop had been cut, the stubble ghostly in the light of the moon that had risen over the rocky outline of the Kankeshwar hills. Nightjars flew up from the road as the cart approached, rattling hoarsely, and owls called from the dark. Now and then they passed a grove of mango trees that were like great black tents pitched in the fields, or an occasional wayside shop in which a single lantern burnt dimly. A dog darted out from one such hovel and raced beside the cart for a while, barking crazily. Then it fell back and there was silence except for the creaking and groaning of the ill-made cart as it lumbered along the road, and Hari lay down and slept.

Let down at the Rewas pier, he was astonished to find it teeming with people. He had not thought so many would be going to Bombay. He had thought he was doing something terribly adventurous – in fact, he found himself trembling with excitement and fear – but here were men and boys of all ages and sizes, dressed in their cleanest clothes, calling and laughing and shouting as they crowded the length of the pier that led into the flat, coffee-coloured sea where fishing boats bobbed up and down wildly, waiting to be loaded.

Adarkar, the organizer from Alibagh, stood at the head of the stairs, shouting orders as the crowd filed down into the boats. Hari too edged his way past the ticket counter that sold tickets for the ferry, the fruit stall where people were buying bananas and sweet limes for the journey, the benches that were empty still, and so to the edge of the pier and the head of the stairs. He hesitated: although he came from Thul, a fishing village, it was a long time since he had been in a boat. Then he heard Adarkar shout, 'Go on, go on – if you are willing to fight for your village and your livelihood, into the boat with you,' and men on either side of him pushed into him so that he was almost lifted off his feet and set down into one of the waiting boats.

By the time the sun was up, turning the dull sea into peacock blue and emerald green and lighting up the city of Bombay on the far shore like a white castle made of sand, or salt, blinding against the hot blue sky, all the boats had been loaded and were setting out like a shoal of dolphins over the waves.

It was fourteen kilometres from Rewas to Bombay. All the way the farmers and fishermen shouted and sang. Their voices rang from boat to boat. They were all in high spirits; it was such a rare outing for them who usually never gave up a day's work to leave their villages, it seemed almost like a holiday. Adarkar had to shout continually to remind them why they were going to Bombay. His voice was getting so hoarse, one of the older fishermen finally tugged at his shirt, hanging out over his *dhoti* and wet with perspiration, and said, 'Sit down, son, sit for a while. Keep your breath for all the shouting you are going to do in Bombay. When we get there we will shout so every man in the city hears us, never you fear. Sit and have a little rest. Give our brother some tea to drink,' he called to the men in the boat. One of them produced a clay cup which was still half full of tea, the rest having spilt earlier. They passed it to their leader who sat down and drank gratefully. Another produced a sweet lime, peeled it and passed him the segments one by one to suck. He was grateful to them and took their advice.

Hari who had bought neither tea nor fruit at the pier nor food from home in the night, sat very quietly on the floor of the boat and no one paid him any attention at all. There was no one else from Thul in his boat; it was full of strangers from other villages along the coast, and he sat listening to them, feeling very tired, hot and thirsty, and very afraid of the journey he had undertaken without thinking at all, simply because he had been upset and angry and simply could not bear to live another day in Thul in the old way. The time for change had come, he had felt that. He had had to make the break he had been thinking about for so long. Had he done wrong?

Of course there was no question of turning back. Having joined this 'procession', there was no way he could back out of it short of leaping into the sea and swimming home. Once in Bombay, he would have to stay, work and earn a living. Was he really ready for that? He felt unsure. He looked back over his shoulder at the flat, marshy coast of Rewas, too far for him to reach. Putting his head down on his knees, he closed his eyes in despair.

'Look at the boy,' someone said. 'Whose son is he? Have you nothing to eat, son?' Here, take this,' and he was handed a cold, dry *chapati*, folded into a triangle. He took it although his throat was so dry he thought he could not possibly chew it or swallow it, but to be polite he bit into it and it gave him a little nourishment and strength.

He needed that for it was the most strenuous day of his life.

He was silenced by awe when he saw the city of Bombay looming over their boats and the oily green waves. He would have liked to stand and stare as he disembarked from the boat at the Sassoon docks, aching and stiff from the long ride in the jam-packed boat, but there was no time, no leisure for that. His fellow passengers were pushing and shoving and jostling past him and he was carried along by them. They pushed and shoved because they were in turn being pushed and shoved by the Bombay crowds that thronged the docks – people in a hurry to get something done, so many people in such a great hurry as the villagers had never seen before. It was only out of the corner of his eye that he saw, briefly, before being pushed on, the great looming sides of steamships berthed at the docks, cranes lifting and lowering huge bales, men bare-bodied and sweating carrying huge packing cases, boxes and baskets on their heads and shoulders, grunting as they hurried, women like the fisherwomen at home with their purple and green saris tucked up between their legs as they ran with baskets of shining, slithering fish from the boats to the market, straw and mud and fish scales making the ground dangerously slippery. Added to this chaos were the smells of the city mingling with the familiar smells of the sea and fish and turning them into something strange, and the noises of the city – not only the familiar fishermen's voices, loud and ringing, but the noise of the traffic which was so rarely heard in or around Thul.

And now they were out through the gates and on the street and in the midst of the terrifying traffic. In all his life Hari had not seen so much traffic as he saw in that one moment on that one street. In Thul there was only an occasional bus driving down the main road of the village to the highway, and very rarely a single, dusty car. When he went to Alibagh, it was chiefly bicycles that he saw, and a few cycle-rickshaws, and of course buses and lorries. But here there was everything at once as if all the traffic in the world had met on the streets of Bombay – cycles, rickshaws, handcarts, tongas, buses, cars, taxis and lorries – hooting and screeching and grinding and roaring past and around him. He clutched the arm of the man next to him in alarm and then was relieved to find it was a farmer from Thul, Mahe.

'Hurry, brother – don't stop – come, we have to go to the *Kala Ghoda,* the Black Horse,' Mahe panted, and together they dodged the traffic and ran straight into a huge red double-decker bus that screeched to a halt just before their noses. The driver leaned out of the window and bellowed at them. They stood transfixed, shaking.

Then the police appeared – the famed Bombay police who, with a wave of their batons and a blast on their whistles, could bring the traffic to a halt or send it up one road and down another, and were capable even of controlling processions and herding marchers through the crowded city such as this one of fishermen from Alibagh.

'Where have you come from, fool?' the policeman roared at Hari. 'Never seen traffic lights? Don't you know how to cross a street? Come straight from the pumpkin fields, have you?'

'Send him back there – let him grow pumpkins – keep him off the Bombay streets,' shouted the bus driver fiercely.

The policeman laughed, held up his hand to keep the bus waiting and waved to the marchers to cross the road.

'We are farmers and fishermen from Alibagh,' said Mahe quietly before he moved on. 'We have come to speak to the Chief Minister.'

'You do that,' the policeman told him. 'You do that – he is waiting for you, with tea and a garland and a sweet for each of you.' He burst out laughing again, winking at the bus-driver as he did so, and then blew his whistle shrilly to make them move. Hari and his companion moved on, very hurt and offended.

'These Bombay-*wallahs*, the rudest people on earth,' muttered Mahe, and Hari nodded.

Those were only the first jeers of the day. They were to hear many more as they walked through the streets to the mysterious Black Horse. As Hari looked up fearfully at the towering buildings, ten and twenty storeys high, at the huge shops and their windows that were as large as the huts at home and much brighter, and pushed past the people who teemed on the streets more plentifully than fish in the sea, he wondered about the Black Horse. Did this amazing city contain a great black horse as a kind of deity, a god? He looked for it eagerly, perhaps a little anxiously, but saw only people, buildings and traffic, and heard only the honking of horns, the grinding of gears and the roar of the great double-decker buses, the taxis and cars. People pushed past with their market bags, handbags and briefcases, grumbling, 'Here's another procession to hold us up,' and, 'What is this lot shouting for now? We'll miss the bus – we'll be late for work – here, get out of my way.'

Once another procession passed directly in front of theirs and they had to stop and wait till it wound past them. To Hari's utter amazement, all the people marching in it were women. They held up banners, raised their fists in the air and shouted, 'Bring down the prices! We want oil! We want sugar! We want rice at fair prices!' and 'Long live Women's Society for Freedom and Justice!' Then all the women would shout in one voice, '*Jail*' and surge forwards. At their head was a grey-haired old lady who waved not her fist but a wooden rolling-pin in the air and all the others laughed and cheerfully encouraged her to hold it high and wave it. Some held cooking pots and beat on them with long-handled cooking spoons, making a great din that they seemed to be thoroughly enjoying.

Hari and the other Alibagh villagers stood open-mouthed in amazement: they had not brought along a single woman with them, had not thought it necessary, had been sure that they, the menfolk, could manage it all on their own and the women would only be a nuisance. Here in Bombay it seemed women did not trust men to manage for them, and they were determined to organize their affairs themselves. It was a very strange new idea to Hari and he did not join in the laughter or the jokes that followed in their wake, but walked on soberly after they had passed, wondering what his mother and Lila would have thought of it.

Now they had the policemen flanking them, waving their batons and keeping them in orderly rows. It seemed they were quite used to such processions and knew exactly how to handle them and direct them. Hari found they were being led around a large circle around which were great domed buildings surrounded by parks and trees. 'Look, look, the museum,' someone cried, and another asked excitedly, 'Will we be able to visit it?' But no, they were being led to a square between large, old, grey office buildings and there, in the centre of the square, was an empty pedestal.

'Black Horse. Black Horse,' Hari heard the men saying and he asked, 'But where is it?' 'Don't you know?' someone said. 'It was taken away when the British left – the people of Bombay did not want to see a foreign ruler after independence, not even a stone one.' 'Oh,' said Hari in gravest disappointment, for he would dearly have liked to see the emperor upon his horse. He stood stock still, staring at the empty pedestal and trying to picture the black horse on it, while the other villagers came to stand beside him. The traffic continued to pour around them as if no one cared why they had come or what they were doing here.

A wooden ladder had been set up beside the pedestal and a thin, elderly man with a white beard, a stranger to the men from Alibagh, climbed on to it. He held a megaphone to his mouth and began to speak. Hari tried to ignore the traffic, the horns blaring and the wheels churning, and to catch a few words of the speech.

'I have come here to speak to you, and speak for you, because I believe in your way of life, because your green fields and the sea are valuable to all of us as they are to you. Our trees, our fish, our cattle and birds have to be protected . . .'

Hari wondered who he was and why he spoke so passionately. He looked like a city man – neat, clean and educated – not like a man from the village used to rough work in the sun and dust. Yet he spoke of fish and cattle and trees with feeling and concern. Why did he care so much?

As if he had heard Hari's thoughts, he answered, 'You may wonder why I, a citizen of Bombay, care to join my brothers from the village and speak in their cause. Maybe you do not trust me to speak for you. In a way, you are right because I do have selfish reasons. All the citizens of Bombay are concerned. These factories that are to come up in Thul-Vaishet will pump deadly chemicals into the air – fertilizer cannot be manufactured without polluting the air for miles around. Sulphur dioxide, ammonia and dust will be scattered far and wide. Recently the ruling government stipulated that no fertilizer complex should be located within fifty miles of big cities. But you know how far Rewas is from Bombay – it is only fourteen kilometres as the crow flies. As it is, Bombay is heavily industrialized, crowded and polluted. How much more pollution can we stand? Do you know that in Japan organic mercury was pumped into the sea, it poisoned the fish and the fish poisoned the people who were unlucky enough to eat them . . .'

Hari strained to listen but the noise of the traffic that was so unfamiliar distracted him. He felt sure the cars and buses were all charging straight at him and if he did not keep a sharp lookout he would be run over. He shifted about uneasily and the men around him bumped into him and talked over his head to each other. The speaker's educated accent was difficult to follow.

'If you are forced to give up farming and fishing, you will have to leave your village and come to Bombay to find work,' he was saying. 'Look around the city now that you are here: is there room for twenty to fifty thousand more people? Do you think there can be enough jobs here, or houses? See how the poor and unemployed live here. Do you wish to change your life in the country amongst your green paddy fields and coconut groves for the life of beggars on the pavements of the city?'

Hari gave a quiver. He felt certain the bearded gentleman was talking to him, questioning him. His mouth fell open with wonder: how did he know Hari had come here to find work? Hari had told no one, he hardly knew his own mind, but this speaker seemed to know more than even he did about himself. 'Who is he?' he asked Mahe who was standing beside him and listening with his mouth open.

'Sayyid – they say his name is Sayyid Ali – something like that,' Mahe answered. 'Not one of the political leaders. Don't know why they've got hold of him to speak to us.'

'He speaks well,' Hari said, 'very well.'

But now he was bowing and climbing down the ladder and a small man in a faded cotton bush-shirt and with wire-rimmed spectacles on his nose was climbing up gingerly to take his place. He was handed the megaphone and began to speak in a squeaky, high-pitched voice. Not only was his voice difficult to follow but Hari could not understand what he was talking about – it was all new and strange. How did these strangers, these city people, know more about Thul and the other fishing villages of the coast than he himself did? He felt more ignorant than he had ever felt in his life.

'You have come from Alibagh,' the man began, 'a place that means home to you, but to us who work in the meteorological observatory, it means the home of the world-renowned Alibagh geomagnetic observatory, the only one of the type in the world. It was established here in Bombay in 1841, not far from where you are standing, but in 1904 it was shifted to Alibagh because Bombay decided to electrify its tram service which would have created a disturbance in the readings of the observatory . . .'

'Huh?' grunted Mahe, lifting his turban to scratch his head. 'What is all this observe-nobserve he is talking about?'

'Don't know,' whispered Hari, trying to hear and learn.

'Now if the fertilizer factory is built near Alibagh, the electric currents and large masses of iron that are brought into the neighbourhood will again vitiate the magnetic observations.'

Hari frowned. He understood less and less.

'We supply information to the Survey of India and to the ONGC – the Oil and Natural Gas Commission. It is essential that our functioning is not disturbed or interrupted. It has been uninterrupted since 1846. We cannot allow it to break down now.' His voice broke and he gulped and stopped to mop his brow with a large handkerchief. One could see this man was used to working in an office, not to speaking at public meetings. 'We – you – all of us should be proud of it. It must be – er – preserved at all cost.' Then he gave up the megaphone and stumbled down into the crowd which applauded out of relief that the speech was over. The speaker himself was smiling weakly with relief.

'Who is he? What is he trying to tell us?' everyone was saying to each other.

'Have you seen this observatory in Alibagh?' someone asked. 'I don't know where it is.'

'Yes, yes, it is a small white house by the sea – I know it,' said another sagely. 'But I did not know it was so important.'

'World-renowned, he said.'

'It must be if he says it is.'

'Yes, yes, very important,' they nodded, impressed.

But another young man, large and hefty, shouted over their heads, 'Preserve a rotten old observatory just because it is so old? What about our farms, our crops, our boats? That is what we have come here to see about – not that man's dusty old office or his files or his job.'

'Yes, yes, that too,' an older man placated him. 'Here, have a smoke, then we will see about our land and boats.'

Now a third man mounted the pedestal. It was their own leader, Adarkar, and so they cheered him loudly although the heat was beginning to wilt them.

His speech soon revived them because it was in their own village dialect and he spoke of the things they knew best. He repeated all he had already talked of before – the richness of their land, the excellence of their crops, of how these must not be given up or destroyed for the sake of the factories, of how they must not be misled by promises of money or jobs, they were unlikely to get any – and everyone nodded and clapped.

'We have come to tell the government we don't want the miserable sums of money they are offering us – our land is too valuable to sell. We are not going to be turned into slaves working in their factories, we have always worked and lived independently and been our own masters. Now let us march to Mantralaya and give our petition to the Chief Minister himself. Let us march, brothers!' and he lifted up his arms and roared the last words.

The roar spread through the whole crowd like a wave surging through it and breaking on the rocks. Suddenly confusion broke out and the crowd began to dissipate and Hari found that the men who had been standing beside him were now drifting away. He hurried first after one group and then after another, wondering where they were going and if he was meant to follow.

Catching the large, hefty young man by his arm, he begged for instructions. 'Do we all have to march to Mantralaya now?'

Just then he heard a voice shout over the megaphone: 'Friends, make your way back to the Sassoon docks where our boats are waiting for us. Only five farmers will go to Mantralaya with the petition. I am one of them. When we have seen the Chief Minister Sahib, we will join you at the docks and travel back together . . .'

'There, you've had your answer,' said the young man, shaking off Hari's hand from his arm and walking off.

Hari stood watching the crowd fade away down the road. He felt deserted and friendless. None of his friends from the village had come – they were the ones who were sitting happily at home waiting for the fertilizer factory to come up and employ them. He had left them to join the march in order to get away from Thul and get to Bombay, and he knew he did not really belong to the march, he had no fields or fishing boats to fight for, nor did he know any of the marchers who were mainly farmers and fishermen, not the sort of people who would know his landless, boatless, jobless father. He felt now that he belonged neither to one group nor the other. He belonged to no one, nowhere. The others had left him behind. He was alone in Bombay.

In the little hut no one gave a thought to the march or even to the launching of Biju's boat. After Hari had run out of the house, the girls had turned to their mother's bed and taken turns at sitting beside her through the night, giving her sips of water to drink and putting damp cloths on her forehead. Sometimes Bela or Kamal, half asleep, would murmur, 'Is Hari back?' and Lila would shake her head silently.

They were all so worn out by that long night that they fell fast asleep just before the sun came up. There was no Pinto today to rush out into the dewy grass and chase the heron into the marsh, barking. Even Lila slept with her head on the edge of her mother's bed, quite forgetting about the rock in the sea or her usual dawn prayers.

Waking up, she was aghast to see how bright it was. The white morning light was a shock, and so was Pinto's silence and Hari's strange disappearance. She thought he must surely have come back in the night after walking off his anger but he was nowhere around. She frowned a little as she got up, then turned immediately to see her mother and the pale, still figure on the bed, still burning with fever, drove every other thought and worry out of her head.

'Kamal, Bela,' she told her sisters when she had woken them up and given them tea. 'Go to the bazaar and get some ice for Ma. See if Hari is there. Call him, he may have stayed in the village at night to see the drama in the temple. Tell him to come home and bring some ice.'

The girls found a few coins on the kitchen shelf and set off down the beach at a run, not even stopping to watch the efforts being made to launch Biju's boat. In any case, most of the villagers appeared to have lost interest in it – there was hardly anyone there except the boys Biju had hired to control the winches and drag the ropes. Bela and Kamal did not linger but went straight to the ice shop in the market. There they ran into Lila's friend Mina who was carrying home a bag of vegetables.

'Have you heard?' she called to them. 'All the men have set off for Bombay with a petition to the government. Someone told me Hari has gone, too.'

'Hari?' they asked, stopping to stare at her. 'Hari gone to Bombay? Oh no, of course not – he must be here somewhere.'

'Where? I haven't seen him. You can ask Raju – he's the one who told me.'

'No, we have to buy ice for Ma. We have to run, she has fever,' they cried, and hurried on.

When they got home they found Lila had just finished burying Pinto in a shallow ditch she had dug behind the frangipani tree. She was smoothing the earth and tramping it down. When she heard them come running up the path, she got up from her knees and dusted her hands and her sari. The girls stopped and watched silently as she walked back to the veranda and sat down slowly on the steps. They could see she had been crying and did not know what to say to console her. They felt their eyes swim with tears as well.

Then Bela gulped and said, 'Lila, Mina says Hari has gone to Bombay with the other men. Raju told her.'

Lila frowned as if she could not understand. Could Hari have been so angry and so upset as to leave home and run away? She could not understand that; she would never have run away herself. She shook her head. It was all very frightening and difficult but she was here, her sisters and her mother were in her care, and somehow she would have to manage. Without saying a word, she got up and went into the house. If Hari was not here, she would go herself to Alibagh to see a doctor and fetch medicine for her mother. Her mother could not get into a bus and go so she would describe everything to the doctor and ask for help. She sighed, thinking how much easier it would have made things if Hari had been here and could be sent to Alibagh instead.

As she was getting ready to go, there was a commotion outside – the unfamiliar sound of a motor roaring up the narrow lane and then the astonishing sight of a car bumping over the grass to the white bungalow, *Mon Repos*.

'Oh, Bela, Kamal, look!' cried Lila. 'The de Silvas have come from Bombay!'

7

FOR SEVERAL hours Hari wandered around the Black Horse, not daring to leave it since this was the only place he had come to know. The villagers had melted away down the many roads that led back to the docks. No one had asked him to come with them, no one had noticed him at all. He was left behind.

Now that he was alone he became aware that he was dreadfully thirsty. He saw a man sitting beside a barrow heaped with coconuts in front of one of the large buildings around the square, and he went towards him, feeling in his pocket for the few coins he had brought with him. 'How much?' he asked. Never having bought a coconut before – at home he could climb a tree and bring down a whole bunch whenever he wanted – he had no idea of the price and nearly fainted when the man said, 'Two rupees.' The man had a sharp, blackened face and spoke from around a cigarette, but when he saw Hari's face, he laughed in quite a kind way. 'What's the matter? Don't you know how much these things cost in a city? No, I can see you don't. Here, I'll find you a cheaper one,' and he searched in the pile for a small coconut and cut off the top with one blow of his curved knife and handed it to Hari. While Hari drank, he watched, amused, and said, 'You look as if you haven't eaten or drunk all day.'

'I haven't,' Hari admitted, wiping his mouth and reaching for the top of the coconut with which to scoop out the sweet white flesh and eat it. 'I am hungry and thirsty.'

'I can see that,' nodded the coconut man. He had no other customers at that time of day and could chat a little with the youngster. 'Run away from your village, have you?'

'I came with the procession,' Hari said proudly. 'You saw the procession that was here just now? We came from Alibagh this morning.'

'Oh? To ask the government for what – food, palaces, jewels?'

Hari tried to explain what their demands were but the coconut seller did not seem to be very interested. Lighting another cigarette, he only said, 'Ask, ask, ask the government all you like. Do you think the government has ears and can hear? Do you think the government has eyes and can see? I tell you, the government has only a mouth with which it eats – eats our taxes, eats our land, eats the poor. Take my advice and keep clear of the government. Don't ask it for anything, don't depend on it for anything. They tell you the government is your father and your mother. I tell you my father and my mother threw me out when I was six years old to go and earn my own living. I don't need them – I fend for myself – I'm a man and depend on myself. That is the best way to be, boy – free and independent. Don't say please and don't say thank you – take what you want. Be a man, be independent.'

Hari listened and nodded. He thought the coconut seller was wise, strong and admirable. He was ready to sit at his feet and learn more but the man did not seem to be interested in teaching Hari: he did not want a pupil or a follower any more than he wanted a father or a mother. He had turned to cut open coconuts for a young man and a woman who came laughing down the steps from the big building and stopped before his barrow, feeling for money in the bags they wore slung from their shoulders. Hari knew he ought to move his rags and his starved face out of the way.

As he moved on down the pavement, walking slowly and carefully to avoid all the filth that was scattered on it in piles and puddles, he heard a voice say, 'Don't listen to that Billu. Keep away from him; he is dangerous. By day he uses his knife on coconuts but by night he uses it on –' and turning around, Hari saw the speaker, a beggar seated on a tattered mat, draw his finger across his throat and stick out a betel-stained tongue to show Hari what he meant. Hari was so startled that the beggar laughed, opening his mouth wide and showing that all of it was stained red with betel juice.

'Are you surprised? Don't you know that is how the people of the pavements live? A safe job as a front to fool the police, and a dangerous one behind it with which to make a living? Do you think a man can keep body and soul together by selling coconuts or by begging? I tell you, he can't. If you want some tips on how to make your way in the city, ask me and I'll tell you – for a small fee,' he added, winking and moving to one side of the mat to make room for Hari.

But Hari had no wish to learn such dangerous tricks from anyone and walked on hurriedly, shaking his head. He did not see the beggar laugh and take out a bottle from under his rags and lift it to his mouth to drink. He had not come to the city to be a beggar, crook or murderer. He did not really know what he had come for except to run away from home and find out what the future held for him. Now he was in Bombay at last and he would find out.

He began to feel afraid of this huge square with its dangerous characters lurking in every shadow, as it seemed. Even the empty pedestal began to look ominous, the absence of the emperor's statue a kind of message for Hari. His fear gave him the courage to turn down a side street and hurry away from it. He saw a long, broad park lined with palm trees and thought he would go and sit on the grass in their shade to rest, watching the footballers and cricketers play, but when he got close, he saw ahead of him, at the end of the road, the bright glitter that he recognized as coming off the sea. He could smell the sea, too, and a powerful whiff of fish.

Suddenly very homesick and longing for something familiar, he forgot about the park and hurried on. When he got to the sea he found that the road curved around the bay in a great swoop. It was the grandest sight Hari had ever seen and he stood staring at the large buildings that lined one side of the road, side by side and taller than trees, and at the sea that lay across the road from them, calm and shining and bright as polished metal. There were no boats and no fishermen here, though, only the traffic pouring down the road and along the sea with a continuous roar.

He walked along between the sea and the buildings till he came to a small sandy beach so crowded with people and stalls of coloured drinks, coconut and food that it was more like a fairground than a beach. In fact it looked as if a fair were on right then – there were balloons held up on bamboo poles, pavement stalls selling flower garlands, plastic toys and magazines, excited children running across the sand to the sea, and people crowding around the stalls and eating strange food that Hari had never seen at home. As he stood on the edge, staring, a car stopped behind him and a large family burst out with cries and shouts of delight – children in bright clothes, women in lovely saris and men who laughed and led them to the stalls to buy snacks and toys.

Seeing them, Hari suddenly remembered that he had in his pocket a piece of paper with the Bombay address of the de Silvas who had offered him a job once. The relief of remembering that he had an address in Bombay and knew people who might help him flooded him like a wave from the sea, cool and friendly and refreshing.

Turning to the nearest stall-owner, a man who was selling balls of ice on which he sprinkled colour and essence – rose, banana, orange and lime – before handing it to excitedly clamouring children, Hari asked him if he knew the address on the piece of paper.

'Oh ho,' laughed the man, rolling his eyes at him comically from under a small white cap. 'Very good address you have there, boy. You must be a prince in disguise.' He held out a bright green ice ball to a child, pocketed some coins and then told Hari, 'Go straight on up the road. It will take you to the top of Malabar Hill and there you will find your palace, just short of the Hanging Gardens. Perhaps there is a princess waiting for you with a garland,' he laughed, and winked.

Hari did not like his laughter or his joke and walked off with as much dignity as he could, his face as serious as always but his heart pounding with excitement.

The road swooped uphill as the man had said it would, with great houses crowding either side of it, beyond which he could see the trees and terraced gardens of a park. The city was bigger and grander than anything he had ever imagined, and he could hardly believe that in it there was a house where people lived who knew him.

His hopes did not last very long. It was evening: the sun sank rose-red into the bay, darkness fell upon the city that was built on an island in the sea. The lights came on as he climbed and the whole hill glittered like a great mound of jewels against the sky, quite outshining the stars. Looking back, he could see the road swooping down and around the bay, lined with a double row of electric lights. Was this the famous Queen's Necklace of which he had heard? He supposed it must be. As he gazed, the neon advertisements above him winked on and off and flared green and blue and orange. His heart beat with excitement and dread.

It was night when he at last found the building he was looking for, but it was not really dark: all the lights along the streets and the hundreds of lights that shone out of the windows of every building made it as light as day, almost. He had never seen so many lights in all his life. It was not like any night he had known and he wished it were darker so that he could hide and not be seen as he walked into the entrance hall of the tall white building called Seabird.

He had of course thought that the family he knew lived in it alone but it was as crowded with strangers as a bus depot or a wharf. A man stood at an inner door letting people in and then shutting it so that they disappeared abruptly. Then, as suddenly, the door was flung open again and quite a different crowd poured out. Hari could not understand it but when he asked the man if the family he knew lived there, the man said, 'Get in – tenth floor,' and he was pushed into a tiny cell along with a dozen other people. The door was shut on them, the man pressed a button in the wall and the little wooden cell shot upwards with a sickening lurch. Before Hari could get over the shock, it had come to a stop, the door was flung open and the man waved him out. 'Number one hundred and two,' he said, shut the door and disappeared.

Now Hari was in the heart of the building. He looked about him and saw nothing but shut doors. He went up close to them to study the numbers and finally found one that had 102 on it in brass letters. He banged and hammered on it for quite a while before it was opened by a tall man in white trousers and a high-collared white coat. 'Why are you banging, idiot – don't you see the bell?' he shouted.

Hari looked up to see if there were a bell hanging from the lintel but there was nothing there. 'No,' he said in a low voice, 'where is it?'

'Here, fool,' said the man angrily and, putting his finger on a white button beside the door frame, made it scream suddenly and shrilly. 'Who are you and what do you want?'

'I want to meet the Sahib,' Hari whispered, staring past the man into the brightly lit room with its carpeted floor, large pieces of furniture and bright pictures and mirrors and flowers. He became conscious of his dirty feet in their dusty sandals and wondered how he could ever step into that room in such a condition.

The man at the door had no intention of letting him do so. 'The Sahib? Who sent you to meet him? Have you a letter?'

Hari felt in his pocket for the bit of paper. 'Here, I have his name and address.'

'Who gave it to you?'

'He gave it to me.'

'Don't tell lies.'

'It is true. When he came to Thul, I washed and cleaned his car for him, and he told me to come and see him when I came to Bombay.'

'Thul?' The man frowned: the name seemed to mean something to him. Hari watched his face hopefully but what he said was another blow.

'The Sahib is not here. He has gone to Thul, where you come from – he left this morning. They have all gone – for their summer vacation. When they come back, the Sahib will go abroad. He is a big businessman, don't you know? He has business in England, in America. He will not come back for another month.' He studied Hari closely. 'So you come from Thul, do you? The cook and ayah have told me about it – a jungly place, they say. What are you doing here?'

'I am looking for work,' Hari whispered. 'I wish to stay.'

This seemed to annoy the man, even frighten him. 'Go, go away,' he shouted. 'There is no work for you here – the Sahib has plenty of servants already. He doesn't need another one – not a boy from Thul certainly. Go – there is no work and nowhere for you to stay,' he repeated harshly and, stepping back, shut the door firmly.

There was nothing Hari could do. He would certainly not press the button and make that loud ringing sound, nor did he dare to bang on the door again. He stood staring at it wretchedly, wondering what to do next and where to spend the night, when the man who had brought him here in the small wooden box that flew, suddenly flung open the door, shouted, 'Coming down? Anyone coming down?' and Hari turned and rushed into the box that dropped at rocketing speed and landed him in the crowded, brightly-lit hall again.

Here he stood, wondering where he could go next, and asking himself why he had ever come to this frightening, friendless place when a man who sat on a high stool by the entrance called him, saying, 'What do you want? Who have you come to see?'

'They are not here,' Hari said, shaking his head. 'They have gone – the family at 102.'

The man paid him no more attention, he was busy talking to people who came and went and shouting at some small boys who were playing marbles on the stairs where everyone bumped into them and tripped on the marbles. The man shouted at them to go and play elsewhere but he had a friendly gleam in his eyes and they laughed at him. Much later, when the hall was emptier, he turned and saw Hari still standing in the corner and walked across to him.

'Haven't you got anywhere to go?' he asked.

Hari shook his head without speaking – he was too tired, too hungry, too weak and frightened to move or speak.

'Hmm,' said the man and stared at him ruminatively. Then, 'Tell you what,' he said with unexpected friendliness. 'I go off duty in half an hour when the night watchman takes over from me. I'm going down to Gowalia Tank where I live. I'll take you along to a friend of mine who will give you a meal. You're hungry, aren't you?'

Hari gazed at him, hardly daring to believe that someone could be kind or helpful. The man put his hand out and patted him on the shoulder. 'Wait a bit,' he said.

His name was Hira Lal and he had been watchman of Seabird for twelve years, he told Hari as they walked downhill late that night, finding their way across the roads and through the traffic and past the big shops and restaurants till they came to the foot of the hill. Here, in a row of small, mean shops, there was a cheap restaurant run by Hira Lal's friend, Jagu. Jagu was to give him a cheap meal and let him sleep there at night. 'I come past this way every night and I will look in on you tomorrow,' he told Hari and walked off with a wave of his hand.

Jagu, who was serving his customers with bread and a watery curry of lentils on tin plates, glanced at Hari and handed him a plate of food without a word. He did not look as pleasant as the well-dressed, good-natured watchman of Seabird – in fact, he was hardly dressed at all and had nothing on but a dirty *lungi* wrapped around his waist, while his chest and back were bare and sweating – but Hari could see that he was a generous man and he sat down with his plate and bent his head over it to eat quickly and hungrily his first meal of that long, exhausting day. When he had finished wiping up the plate with bits of bread, Jagu came and tossed him another *chapati* and Hari ate that, too: he was so hungry. He was not used to very much better food at home, after all, and he had never been so hungry in his life, or so tired.

When Jagu waved his hand and indicated that he should lie down on one of the long wooden benches to sleep after the last customers had left, Hari did so at once and although the bench was hard and the noise and the light from the street came streaming in, he slept at once, and soundly.

8

HARI had been so tired and weak and anxious that first night that he had not really been aware of the place in which he found himself. He only saw it for the first time when he woke next morning.

The Sri Krishna Eating House was the meanest and shabbiest restaurant Hari had ever seen: even in Thul and along the Alibagh–Rewas highway there were cafés that were pleasanter; usually wooden shacks built in the shade of a mango or frangipani tree with a handful of marigolds and hibiscus crammed into an old ink bottle for a vase, coloured cigarette packets and bottles of aerated drinks attractively arranged on the shelves, and possibly a bright picture of a god or goddess on the wall with a tinsel garland around the frame and heavily scented joss sticks burning before it.

But the Sri Krishna Eating House of Gowalia Tank, Bombay, did not have even so much as a coloured picture of Krishna cut out of a magazine and glued to the wall. Or perhaps there had been one and it had disappeared under the layers and layers of grime and soot with which the walls were coated. The ceiling was thick with cobwebs that trapped the soot and made a kind of furry blanket over one's head. The floor and the wooden tables were all black, too, since they all got an even share of soot from the open stoves in the back room where the lentils were cooked all day in a huge aluminium pan and the *chapatis* were rolled by hand and baked.

It was certainly the cheapest restaurant anyone could possibly find in Bombay – even a beggar could afford to buy himself a meal here, and the usual customers were beggars and coolies who had stopped in between carrying their loads – sacks of coal and cylinders of gas – and cart-pullers who dragged goods through the city on long wooden hand-drawn carts. These people seemed to have no fixed working hours – before daylight there were some waiting for a meal who were given the leftovers of the night before, and the last came in after midnight when the whole city seemed to collapse into exhausted, disturbed sleep. So of course the owner had no time to sweep or clean his restaurant or the money to decorate it with pictures and flowers.

He worked hard himself all day and had two boys to help him knead the dough in huge pans, roll out the *chapatis* and bake them over open fires which they kept lit day and night.

When Hari said next morning – after being handed a tumbler of tea and a rolled up chapati without his asking for anything – 'I have no money to pay for all this food you are giving me. Will you let me work in your kitchen instead?' the man considered for only a moment, frowning as he thought. Then he said, 'Yes, I can do with another boy in the kitchen. Start by washing these pots. Then you can knead the dough and help roll out the *chapatis*. If you like, you can stay here and work for your meals and – uh – one rupee a day, like the other boys.'

So Hari went to work in the small kitchen at the back of the eating house. He saw there was nothing to scour the pots with except some blackened coconut husks and the ash from the fires, and he did the best he could with them although Lila would certainly not have considered the results good enough. Later he helped the two boys knead great hills of dough in their pans and this was hard work and made them grunt and sweat. They did not speak to each other as they worked. When the boys finally did say something to each other, Hari realized it was in Tamil, a language he did not know. Nor did they seem to know any Hindi or Marathi, the two languages he knew, so there was silence between them. They were in any case neither friendly nor inquisitive about him, or else they were simply too tired and too sad to speak. They built up the fires and then while one rolled out the *chapatis*, the other baked them over the fire with a pair of long tongs, and Hari was given the task of carrying them out to the customers eating at the long tables in the front room. There was so much work and such heat in that small place that no one ever seemed to have the strength or the time to talk. Hari, too, fell silent.

He would have had to remain silent if the man in the shop next door had not proved friendlier. It was a watch repair shop with its name painted on a signboard over the door: *Ding Dong Watchworks*, and when Hari came out to empty a pail of garbage into one of the big concrete disposal units built on the roadside, the man who stood at the counter, wearing a small black cap and with an eyepiece fixed to his eye, working at a minute watch that he held in the cup of his hand, looked at him and smiled. Hari smiled back. The old man looked so much like Sayyid Ali, the man who had spoken so well at the meeting by the Black Horse, that Hari instantly felt here was another fine and impressive man whom he could trust and who would understand him and try to help him.

'So, a new boy at the Sri Krishna Eating House,' called the old gentleman, then went back to his examination of the tiny watch, but continued to talk to Hari who stood on the pavement, staring open-mouthed at all the clocks that hung tick-tocking on the walls and the watches that glittered in the show cases. 'New to the city?' he asked in a high-pitched, rather cracked and reedy voice.

Hari nodded yes.

'Where do you come from? Jagu's village?'

'Oh no, I don't know Jagu at all. I come from Thul which is near Alibagh,' Hari said eagerly, finding the words rushing out like the small waves of the sea, brightly and happily. He felt proud of that address. Sayyid Ali of the Black Horse would have understood why but it was obvious this gentleman knew nothing of Alibagh; he looked puzzled and curious. 'It was the watchman of a big building on a hill who brought me here to eat – and I have stayed, to work.'

'Other people have come to Jagu for help.' The old man nodded, poking about the watch's mechanism with a long fine needle. 'He is a silent man, never speaks to anyone – but he has been good to many. Like those two boys who work for him: their parents were killed in a railway accident; they were all living on a railway platform as many do who come to the city to find work, and one day a train ran over the parents as they were crossing the line to fetch water from a pump. There's the station where it happened,' he waved his fine, yellow hand with the long needle in it down the street and then continued: 'That's when Jagu found the boys as he was coming to work in the morning, and he brought them here straight away and gave them food and shelter and work, too.'

Hari was shocked by the story but he did not like to be thought of as another orphan in Jagu's care. He did have parents after all – even if one was a drunkard and the other an invalid – and a home, a proper home, not just a place on a railway platform. Thinking of them, he suddenly said, 'Sir, can you tell me where the post office is? I wish to buy a postcard.'

'Ah-ha,' laughed the old watchmaker, winking at him from behind the eyepiece. 'Suddenly remembered you had someone to write to, did you? Yes, you must write. Of course you must write. Go straight up the road and on your left, next to the electric substation, there is a post office. Have you money for a post card or can I lend you some?'

Hari gratefully took the coin from him, promising to return it as soon as Jagu paid him his salary, and then hurried off to the post office. Having bought the card, he had to have a pen to write with and for this he returned to the watchmaker who seemed more likely to have one than the owner of the eating house. This was in the middle of the sweltering afternoon when there was no one in the shop, and even the two orphans had fallen asleep under the table, from heat and exhaustion. Hari sat on the steps of the *Ding Dong Watchworks* and carefully wrote with a ballpoint pen that the old watchmaker lent him:

> Dear Mother,
> I am in Bombay. I have a job. I will bring you my earnings. I hope you are well. I am well. Remember me to my sisters.

Then he wrote his name in large letters to fill up the space, but not his address, and went off to post it, feeling both happy to have done what he knew he should do and frightened because this meant he would be staying on in Bombay, not going home.

Bela and Kamal came running out to stand beside Lila and watch the de Silvas piling out of their car. The cook was already walking towards the hut, calling from the other end of the log that lay across the creek, startling the old grey heron that stood hunched on a stone and making it flap away into the grove of casuarinas and pandanus.

'Where is that brother of yours?' called the cook. 'Tell him to come and help carry the luggage into the house.'

'He's not here,' Lila started to say, then stopped herself, gave Bela and Kamal a little push, whispering, 'Go and help. Carry in their bags – tell them I'm just coming.' She went back to the hut to see if her mother needed anything and to give her a drink of water, then tucked her sari in at the waist and went across the creek to the house to help. Quickly giving up her plan to go to Alibagh for help that morning, she decided she might get more help from the de Silvas – who were rich, and had a car, and could help – and she would try and get it.

After sweeping the house for them, cleaning away the spiderwebs from the corners and fetching water from the well for the kitchen, she asked the old cook who stood watching her and grumpily supervising, 'How long are they going to stay here?'

'A whole fortnight, they say,' he grumbled. 'It is their holiday season – the schools are closed – and instead of going abroad, they want to spend a fortnight here first. I don't know how we'll manage in this wilderness. Where are the shops? I asked them. Your brother used to do the shopping for us – now you tell me he isn't here. Where will we get bread and fresh eggs and vegetables from? I don't know how I'm supposed to manage – but manage I must while *they* enjoy themselves.' He glanced at the family who were carrying cane chairs and cushions out under the coconut trees while the children ran about with toy buckets and spades and rubber balls.

Lila sat back on her heels and stared at the cook. 'My sisters and I will help. We can go to the bazaar and fetch anything you need. We get almost everything in Thul but sometimes your sahib can drive to Alibagh in the car and buy what you can't get here.'

'Yes, that is how it will have to be done,' he grumbled. 'Here are the vegetables for lunch – start washing and peeling them. In the evening will you go and get some fish? And what about bread for tomorrow's breakfast?'

'I will get you fresh fish on the beach when the fishing fleet comes in,' Lila promised. 'There is some bread here in our bazaar but if you want factory-made city bread, perhaps your sahib can drive to Alibagh to buy some.'

'He will have to – I'll just go and tell him,' said the cook.

But Mr de Silva did not feel like getting back into the car and driving to the next town when he had only just arrived and was relaxing after the long, dusty drive. He had already stripped to his bathing trunks and was setting off down the beach for a swim. The rest of the family, in their bathing clothes, were already jumping in the waves that splashed over them and screaming and laughing. Their beautiful golden dog raced up and down the beach, barking and throwing up sand and racing away from the waves as they came foaming towards him.

The cook stood watching and growled, 'Look at them. Is this what they come all the way here for? They can bathe at home, more comfortably. But they're mad, that's what they are – mad.'

But the next day, when the bread ran out, Mr de Silva had to get into the car and fetch more. He said to the cook, 'Tell me all you need and I'll go and do your shopping in Alibagh today so you won't need to bother me again.'

Hearing this, Lila darted out from the kitchen, stood before him with her hands clasped before her and her eyes cast down shyly, and asked what she had made up her mind to ask: 'Sahib, can you take my mother to the hospital in Alibagh? If you are going in the car, may she and I go with you? She has been so ill and there is no doctor and no hospital here.'

Mr de Silva looked shocked and stammered a bit, not knowing what to say, but his wife came running down the veranda and stood listening to Lila. 'Why didn't you tell me she was ill?' she asked. 'I always bring some medicines with me – I might have been able to help.'

Lila looked at her with gratitude and explained, 'She has been ill for so long – she has grown very thin and weak. I don't know what medicine to get for her. A doctor must see her. There is a hospital in Alibagh. I thought – I thought if you can take her there – and I'll work for you – then the money you pay me – uh – that can pay for the doctor and the medicine.'

'Of course!' exploded Mr de Silva. 'Of course we will pay for the medicine. Go and fetch your mother.'

That was a day of such excitement that Lila might have enjoyed it if it had not been for all the strain and worry that went with the excitement. She had hardly ever been to Alibagh before although it was only three kilometres away, and certainly never before sat in a motor car. Yet when she did so, she could only worry about her mother who lay stretched out on the back seat, moaning, with her head on Lila's lap, looking so pale and sick that Lila wondered if she would reach Alibagh alive. She was so occupied with holding her mother's head and keeping her covered with a sheet that she did not look out of the window at the road or the trees or the bullock carts and bus stops that they passed. Mr de Silva drove at great speed as if he too were afraid he might not get Lila's mother to the hospital in time, and in a short while they were driving up the wide, quiet road to the hospital.

Here Lila began to feel so helpless that she would not have known what to do if Mr de Silva had not been with her and helped her. 'Wait here – I'll go and fetch a stretcher and a nurse and go and speak to a doctor,' he said through the back window and then marched off with the purposeful stride of a city man past the rows of patiently waiting villagers in the compound.

He made all the arrangements and in a little while two men in white came with a stretcher and rolled Lila's mother gently on to it and carried her in. Lila ran after them with a little bundle made up of a shawl, a towel, a comb and a metal tumbler. Then she ran up the steps and down the veranda after her, following her into a ward where the beds stood in a double row under the slowly revolving electric fans. The room was cool and darkened by the green paint on the window-panes. The stretcher bearers lifted her mother on to one of the beds and a nurse came hurrying forwards to make her comfortable.

'Wait here – I'll speak to the doctor, then I'll take you home,' said Mr de Silva, and Lila nodded and sat down beside the bed, trembling with fear and nervousness.

'Don't look so frightened,' smiled the nurse as she straightened the sheets and arranged things on a small table by the bed. 'We will look after her – we have very good doctors – you needn't worry now.'

The doctor came and examined Lila's mother who had not opened her eyes or spoken but lay still and white under the sheet. Lila stood biting her lip and watching the doctor and trying to understand what he said to Mr de Silva in English. At last he turned around and spoke to her in Marathi. 'Leave her here with us. It will take a long time to cure her, she is so emaciated. We will have to get many tests done to begin with, to find out what is wrong. That will take some days. We will send you the report – or you can come and fetch it after a week. But don't worry – there is nothing wrong that we can't put right.'

Lila shook her head: she did not want to leave her mother. But Mr de Silva said, 'You have your sisters at home – you must come. I will bring you back after a few days, I promise. Come along.'

She was not brave enough to argue with him, so she followed him to the car but wept all the way home.

That night when her father was leaving the hut, he stopped to stare at her while she tried to light a fire with some sticks, and growled, 'Where's your mother gone?'

'I took her to the hospital in Alibagh,' Lila whispered, still on her knees and not daring to look up.

There was a dangerous roaring sound as he swayed on his feet above her like a tree about to fall. His shadow on the wall was made huge as a giant's by the small flickering flames of the fire. 'Why did you send her away without asking me?' he roared.

'You were – you were asleep, Father,' Lila whispered.

There was another roar from him. 'I will go to her,' he shouted. 'Why did you take her away without telling me? I will go to Alibagh – I will find her. She can't be left alone, you stupid girl.'

'The nurses and doctors will look after her, Father,' Lila cried, afraid he would go to the hospital and make a drunken scene.

'Don't answer back, girl,' he shouted. 'What do you know about anything? What makes you think you can manage things? You can't.' He kicked over an earthen waterpot in his rage so that it fell and broke with a crash, flooding the kitchen floor. This made him even angrier and he stamped on the pieces of clay, smashing them to bits while he shouted, 'How could you leave her alone? What if she needs something? What if she asks for me? Did you think of that?' He picked up one of the pots on the shelf and hurled it on the floor beside Lila who cowered. 'Cook some food, quick – I will take it to her.'

'It's late, Father,' said Lila, crying.

'It's not late – don't answer back,' he shouted, sweeping off a whole row of tumblers from the shelf. 'Make the food at once. I'm going to take it to her at Alibagh,' he roared and began to crash around the house, hurling things about, while Lila hastily began to roll out the *chapatis* and bake them, although tears ran from her eyes and blinded her.

There was so little in the house to cook but she made up a small bundle of food and gave it to her father who went storming down the path in the dark, cursing all of them as he went, waking up all the stray dogs of Thul and making them howl.

Suddenly Lila remembered something. Snatching up the lantern from its hook on the kitchen wall, she ran out to the log on the creek and called, 'Father! If – if the Khanekar brothers come again to ask for money – what shall I do?'

She could not make out her father's face or expression in the dark but she could see him halt for a moment. Then he swayed, waved his arm about his head, and roared, 'Do? Tell them to get off my land, that's what.'

'Father,' she cried, in a trembling voice, 'last time they killed Pinto because they said you owed them money for toddy –'

'That's a lie! I owe no one money,' he roared, swaying about in the pandanus grove like a ghost. Then, in a slightly lowered voice, he called, 'I will stop by their house and pay them. I will tell old Hira-*bai* to look after you girls till your brother comes back. Curse him, where is that rascal?' Muttering, he went crashing through the grove to the Khanekars' house.

Lila stood listening tensely for sounds of a quarrel, but there were none. Of course, she realized, at this time of night, the brothers would not be at home, they would be out drinking. Probably only old Hira-*bai* was at home and she was certainly not as bad as the men. So she went back to the hut, feeling sure her father would go straight on to the toddy shop for his customary drink.

He did not, however, come back the next day or the next. When Mr de Silva took Lila to visit her mother and collect the reports, she was frightened to find him sitting on the veranda outside her mother's ward. He got to his feet when he saw them coming and stood in the doorway silently when Lila went in. As she passed him, she noticed that for once he did not smell of toddy. He looked so grey and old and bent that for the first time she felt sorry for him. Then she went in to see her mother and found her in bed but awake, washed and clean.

The nurse stopped and smiled at her. 'See, she is still here, your mother – we haven't hidden her away. Doesn't she look better? She is taking her medicine and she is better already.'

Lila sat and held her mother's hand, smiling in relief. Her mother smiled back at her silently.

It was Mr de Silva who went to the doctor to collect the reports and explained them to Lila as they drove home. 'She is suffering from anaemia. A very bad case of it, the doctor says. It is lucky we brought her here in time. They have done many tests – X-rays and blood tests and so on – and they found that she has a touch of TB too, just a slight one that they can cure with medicines. They are giving her injections and good food, and she will get well. Of course it will take time – they say you must leave her with them for some time. Your father has said he will stay and look after her. Is that all right?'

Lila, who sat awkwardly in the back, not used to the slippery seat or the swaying motion of the car, had to nod and agree. She could do nothing else although a thousand worries clouded her mind and darkened her face.

Mr de Silva seemed to be watching her in the little mirror that hung over the windscreen. 'Don't worry so much,' he said kindly. 'I have given your father a little money for his food since he wants to stay at the hospital. We are paying for the medicines – the hospital itself is free. You will be paid for the work you and your sisters do for us so you'll have something for running your own household.'

'But – you will go away soon,' Lila mumbled.

'Yes, we are going but a friend of ours is coming from Bombay to live at *Mon Repos* for a few months. He will be alone and he will need a servant to look after him because we are taking ours back with us. If you wash and sweep and cook for him, he will pay you a salary.'

'For a few months?' Lila asked disbelievingly. No one had ever stayed that long at *Mon Repos*. 'But the monsoon will come.'

'Yes, he wants to spend the monsoon at Thul. He is doing a study of – well, you will find out. He is a strange fellow,' chuckled Mr de Silva, and swerved sharply to avoid a bullock cart on the road. When the car went steadily forwards again, he said, 'So stop worrying now – you will have work and you will earn money and your mother will be taken care of at the hospital: your father is there to see to that,' and he began to whistle cheerfully as if every problem had been solved. Lila was not quite so sure about that but she was glad not to have to say any more and to stare silently out of the window at the bare, baked fields as she wondered about the future. Ever since Hari had left, everything had become uncertain.

She thought of Hari with such longing that tears stung her eyes and her fingers curled up in knots. It seemed as if Hari knew that, wherever he was, for when they got out of the car, Bela and Kamal were standing on the log over the creek, waving a yellow postcard in the air and screaming, 'From Hari! Hari has written us a postcard!'

'Hari?' cried Lila, tumbling out of the car and running towards them. 'Where is he? What is he doing?'

9

THE WORK was not easy in that firelit kitchen of the Sri Krishna Eating House that seemed to grow hotter and hotter and never to cool down even at night. The eating house never quite shut and customers had to be served with tea and bread or bread and lentils whenever they demanded it, day or night. Jagu kept his promise of paying Hari a rupee a day which came to seven rupees a week, good wages for a young boy new to the work, and Hari was grateful for it. Since he also got his meals free, he could save all that money to take home to his family, and he was proud of the amount he was collecting for them. What he minded was not being able to leave the eating house and go home when the work was done. He was confined to it day and night: he worked in the kitchen and in the front room, washed and bathed under the tap at the back, ate his meals at the table when there was no customer around, and slept on the bench or sometimes on the dusty black floor. This was the hardest of all.

Outside the traffic ground past all through the night: when the buses had stopped, there were still the hand-drawn carts rattling through the streets with goods from the railway station and warehouses for the markets, and cars and taxis at all hours. When the cinema houses closed after the last show, hundreds of people poured out and streamed past, shouting and blowing paper horns and singing songs from the cinema show. Then the lights were never put out in the city which was always lit up so that Hari's tired eyes longed for the deep darkness and the quiet nights of his seaside village. He could hardly remember the soft sounds of the sea or the wind in the coconut palms or the feel of the clean sand between his fingers and under his feet – it was all so long ago and far away. He had only been away for one season, just the few months between winter and summer, but it seemed like a lifetime.

He would have fallen ill from lack of sleep if he had not one night got up and gone out to sit on the pavement because it was a degree cooler there than in the eating house with its fiery heat and stale smells and stuffy air. The old watchmender, who had stayed late to finish some work on a watch he had promised to have ready, had come over to him after pulling down the steel shutter over his shop and said, 'What's the matter, Hari? Not ill, are you?'

Hari shook his head and said nothing – he was so fuddled by tiredness and lack of sleep.

'Can't sleep in there, eh? Must be terribly hot and stuffy. This is a bad month – May – before the monsoon comes,' he said, sighing, and lifted the black cap off his head to mop his bald pate with a large green handkerchief. 'My room is as bad as the shop – it's on the top floor, you see, in one of those buildings that overlook Grant Road station,' he waved his handkerchief at the busy intersection before folding it and putting it away. 'Tell you what, why don't you go and sleep in the park, eh? Wish I could come too, it will be cooler – but my cat will be waiting for me, my old puss.' He chuckled to himself, quite happily, and wandered off unsteadily.

Hari was always to be grateful to the old watch-mender for this advice for the park changed his life and made it easier to endure. It was only a city park – a dusty square with some patches of worn grass, iron benches, rows of canna lilies and some palm trees – surrounded by very old and shabby buildings – not to be compared with the beach and the coconut grove at home, but still, it had a bench to lie on, trees to look at, some pigeons and crows to watch, and even if the city never seemed to grow cooler and the night air was even staler than by day, used up by the millions of gasping city-dwellers, it was certainly more bearable than the eating house kitchen.

Lying on the wooden planks of the bench, Hari could see the tattered fronds of the dusty palm trees over his head and even one or two of the brightest stars, struggling to shine through the dust and soot of the city. When he got up and put his feet down he felt grass under them, not the hard, cruel city concrete.

The park was watched over by a policeman in khaki, a young man with a fierce, sharp-tipped moustache that he kept twisting as he stood with his baton tucked under his arm, keeping a sharp eye on the people who went in and out of the park. On the first night that Hari lay down on the bench to sleep, he stalked across and growled, 'Get up, boy, go home. This is no place to sleep. Get up quick or I'll take you off to the police station – you can sleep as long as you like there.'

Hari had just felt the luxury of stretching out and putting his feet up after a hard day at the eating house and he sat up, miserable. 'I have nowhere to go,' he said, 'I live here.'

'Nowhere to go? I'll show you where you can go,' bellowed the policeman ferociously, waving his baton over Hari's head, and was about to bring it down with a crack when an old gentleman who happened to be walking by, tapping his walking stick before him, stopped and spoke to the policeman.

'Why bully a poor harmless boy, Mr Mighty Policeman?' he piped in a small, shrill voice like a child's. 'There are enough bad characters in this city – thugs, murderers, thieves, gamblers, drunkards – why not go after them instead? Why not start with those drunkards playing cards in that corner over there? They make life unsafe for us who live in this locality, we are all afraid to come to this park because of them – not because of this poor boy who has no home and nowhere else to sleep,' he said.

The policeman stood chewing his moustache uncertainly. 'Hrumph,' he grunted, not knowing quite what to do. The bent old man had made him feel ashamed of bullying a child when there was adult work to be done: tackling the real criminals of the city. 'Hrumph,' he said again, more loudly. 'Who are these men? Where are they? I'd better go and see,' he said, and went off. The old man gave a little chuckle, winked at Hari, and hobbled off, tapping with his stick.

After that the policeman greeted him every night as he entered the park when his work was done, and Hari felt safe and even quite grand to have a policeman guard him while he slept.

When he opened his eyes in the morning he saw pigeons tumbling in the dirty grey sky. They came whirring down in a flock to alight on the statue in the middle of the park where a man stood throwing handfuls of grain to them, and Hari watched delightedly as they waddled about on their pink claws, pecking and quarrelling. Every morning this man came to scatter grain for the pigeons and Hari watched them come and feed. Then there was an old woman in a widow's white sari who brought a bag of flour to the park and painstakingly sprinkled a pinch of flour on every ant hill along the paths. She herself was like an old white ant, bent and hunched, crawling along with her weak eyes bulging as she strained to find ants to feed. Hari watched her, wondering. He certainly would not have spent his money on feeding birds and ants; he had his family to think of and was saving every rupee he earned for them.

A little later, when he went to the pump in a corner of the shrubbery to wash, he saw the schoolchildren pouring by with their satchels across their shoulders. They all wore the same clothes – grey shorts or skirts and light blue shirts or blouses – faded and mended, and they all had their hair oiled and combed down very flat. Some went by in laughing, racing groups, others had to be led by their mothers or grandparents to the school building at the end of the park. Watching them, Hari thought of his sisters, Bela and Kamal, in their indigo blue skirts, skipping and running down the village road to the school by the hill, and wondered when he would see them again. He wished he had given them his address after all so that they could write and send him news of home.

The boys in the kitchen, now that they knew he was there only to help them and not to take away their work or food, looked at him with less hostility and sullenness. Jagu seemed pleased with Hari, too, and sometimes handed him a glass of tea in the middle of the day or, when he had a few moments to spare, sat down at one of the long wooden tables, drummed loudly on it and sang a song in a dialect Hari did not know, wagging his head to the tune and rolling his eyes. When he caught Hari listening and smiling, he smiled back. Then Hari knew that he too had a village somewhere that he called home, that he remembered it and that the memory made him happy. It was just that he was a silent, hardworked, worried man and had no time and no gift for speech that might have made him a friend as well as a benefactor.

It was the watchmender, Mr Panwallah, who was truly a benefactor, the kindest and most helpful of all. One afternoon, during those hot, still hours when there were no customers for a change, Hari was standing in front of the eating house, idly watching the traffic because he was too tired to do anything else, and Mr Panwallah called to him to come and sit beside him on the bench behind the counter in his shop.

'Want to help?' he asked. 'Want to learn how to make a clock tick? I'm just going to open this big grandfather clock sent me by an old Parsee family for repair – you'll be able to see the workings plain. Don't often get a piece like this any more – wall clocks, yes, and electronic gadgets – but you don't often come upon a grandfather clock like this. It's a real piece of luck, being able to show you one of this size. Look,' he said, swinging open the door at the back and revealing the machinery to a fascinated Hari who felt as if the door had opened into a new and strange house. Mr Panwallah showed Hari what was wrong with it, what had made it stop. 'Interesting, isn't it? How would you like to learn? Tell you what – I'll take you on as an apprentice – in the afternoons, when you don't have to work in the kitchen. You don't have much to do between two and four, do you? Of course you will have to ask Jagu first. I can pay you a little, not much, and you can help me for two hours a day. Perhaps I can make a watchmender of you. That's not a profession many know. How would you like that, eh?'

Hari could not believe that he actually meant that, that he was actually willing to share his secrets with a village boy who was working as a cook's help in a beggars' kitchen. The man's kindness and the possibility that he might make something of his life, learn to put his hands to good use, handle tiny, delicate tools and work upon intricate, complicated machinery, made him feel so dazed that he could not speak and only nodded silently.

'Here, let's start at once so we can see if you have a taste for it,' chuckled the old man, handing him a tiny screwdriver with a green handle like glass.

'My hands are too dirty,' Hari mumbled in shame.

'Dirty, are they?' laughed Mr Panwallah. 'Oh, just wipe them on this towel here. They're all right now.' He seemed delighted to have an apprentice: he enjoyed company as much as Jagu did not. 'You've got clever fingers, I can see. Now here's a useful little tool – hold it like this and I'll show you what to do.'

That was how Hari became an apprentice watchmender and saw that it was possible to have a future, that one did not remain where one was stuck always but could move out and away and on. One needed to make great efforts for this to happen, but it helped to have a little luck as well. He got Jagu's permission to spend the slack afternoon hours at the watchmender's without any trouble – Jagu was taciturn, but good-natured – and he set to learning the craft with a will. He began to brighten up and look happy and alive, and the old watchmender smiled to see him at work, frowning with concentration and eagerness.

'Good, Hari, good,' he said again and again, encouragingly, 'that's very good. By the time the monsoon comes, I'll have finished giving you your first lessons. By the time the monsoon is over, you'll be mending watches on your own.'

Hari looked up at him, silently, grateful for the suggestion that time would pass.

'Yes,' said the old man, looking at him. 'Maybe I'll make you smile at last – or even laugh, eh?'

The visitor who was to stay at *Mon Repos* through the monsoon arrived in Thul the day before the de Silvas left and in the hubbub and confusion, Lila and her sisters did not become aware of his presence immediately. He came on the bus from Bombay and walked down the path, carrying his own bag, and therefore made no grand, impressive entrance. The family was so large and noisy that an extra person in its midst made no difference at all. Only the dog, Misha, seemed to be barking and running around more excitedly than usual.

Lila was busy helping the cook clear the kitchen and pack their belongings. Her sisters went to collect flowers for the memsahib before she left – allamanda and hibiscus and frangipani blossom, and garlands of jasmine for the children. The children were all over the veranda, quarrelling over the shells and pebbles they had collected on the beach and which their mother refused to let them take back to their flat in Bombay. 'At least, not all – you can choose just a few of the best,' she told them, which caused much heartache as they looked through their collections and decided what to take. Bela and Kamal giggled at the sight – they themselves were so used to the shells and pebbles littered on the beach that they hardly noticed them.

At last the luggage was loaded on to the car and the family climbed in, leaning out of the windows to call goodbye to Lila and her sisters.

'Don't you worry about your mother,' Mr de Silva said again and again. 'You leave her in the hospital for the monsoon, d'you hear – it's too wet and damp in your hut during the rains and she is better off in the hospital with your father to keep an eye on her. I'm going to stop in Alibagh to give him some money to keep him going till she is well and they can come back. The doctor thinks he can send her home at Diwali – will that be all right?'

Lila nodded and nodded, grateful to him for repeating what she had already been told but she liked to hear again. It was so quiet in their hut without Hari, without Father or Mother, without even Pinto, and would be even quieter now with the de Silvas gone from *Mon Repos*.

'And look after Sayyid Ali Sahib well,' Mrs de Silva called. 'Be sure to see he eats his meals – it's the sort of thing he forgets to do, so you will have to remember. He is a very great man – take good care of him. I've left enough money with you to give him fish and milk and eggs every day, and he likes vegetables – so get plenty of vegetables. Clean the kitchen every night before you lock it up so that cockroaches and rats and snakes don't come –'

The children on the back seat shrieked for that reminded them of the snake their mother had come upon in the kitchen last night and that had hurriedly disappeared into a cupboard. 'OOOH, snakes!' they screamed, and their father decided this was the time to leave so he started the car and set off with a jolt that made their dog bark wildly with excitement as he hung his head out of the window and saw the coconut trees whirling past him and Lila and Bela and Kamal standing on the log over the creek and waving goodbye.

When the car had gone and they were left standing alone, staring at the suddenly quiet house, they saw who it was who was to stay on at *Mon Repos* – a thin elderly man with a white beard and spectacles on his nose. He did not notice them at all for he had a pair of binoculars glued to his eyes and was staring intently into the trees.

The girls stared at the trees, too, wondering what he was looking at. There seemed to be nothing there but then they heard a rustle and an ashy grey and russet bird flew out, trailing a long russet tail behind it as it came out of the foliage and around to the back of the house. The man lowered his binoculars with a sigh and drew out a book from his pocket and began to scribble in it.

Lila and her sisters tiptoed around the corner and into the kitchen so as not to disturb him.

'What is he doing?' they whispered as they quietly washed the dishes that had been left behind in the sink.

'Who knows?' Lila shrugged. 'He is here to study something, the sahib said.'

'Study what – the *birds*?' asked Bela, and Kamal laughed at the idea, it was so ridiculous.

'Anyway, he won't notice us at all – we just have to cook his meals and call him to come and eat them,' said Lila.

That was what they did. Now they had not their mother to look after, or Hari or their father, they quietly cooked and marketed and swept and washed for the strange gentleman who never spoke to them, only glanced through his spectacles at the food when they called him for his meals, and disappeared for the whole day sometimes, carrying his binoculars over his shoulder and a bag full of books and pencils. Sometimes they ran into him as he stumbled about the marsh, splashing through the mud and reeds, or sitting very quietly on a stone under the trees, staring intently at everything – except people. He seemed hardly to notice that there were any people in Thul; they did not appear to interest him at all. But he was polite and quiet and gave no trouble at all since he had neither complaints nor demands and so they did not mind his oddities or even giggle at them much except once when he stepped backwards off the log into the creek with a splash and they had to run to help him up and to retrieve his bag and papers and spread them out on the veranda to dry. Then they noticed that his papers were covered with careful pencil sketches of birds. They were wonderstruck.

'See, he *is* studying the birds,' whispered Bela as they knelt on the veranda tiles, carefully separating the wet sheets and spreading them out in the sun.

'Studying the *birds*?' whispered Kamal and burst into uncontrollable giggles. But Lila frowned at them and told them to take care, the drawings were so beautiful, they must not spoil a single one.

The strange gentleman came out of his room in dry clothes and stood watching them worriedly. Then, 'Thank you, thank you,' he said gratefully and took some money out of his pocket to give Bela and Kamal. 'For sweets,' he said in a mumble, and hurried away in embarrassment.

He looked just as embarrassed when he paid Lila her salary at the end of the month and she whisked out of sight as quickly as possible, then ran round the house and across the creek to their hut, laughing with joy. It was wonderful to earn money. There was enough now to stock their kitchen with rice and tea and sugar, and Lila went every week to the hospital in Alibagh by bus to take some to their father who bought extra milk and fruits for their mother with it. The money made everything possible and Lila hoped the gentleman would stay on and on so that she could continue to earn money.

'But no one stops in the monsoon,' Kamal said. 'Everyone goes away when the monsoon comes. Only we stay.'

10

'THE MONSOON is coming!' shouted old Mr Panwallah, stepping back from the sea wall as a huge wave came crashing against it, throwing out a whiplash of spray at the crowd collected on the promenade to watch. 'See, Hari, the monsoon is coming!'

Hari nodded, laughing as the spray drenched him. The crowd fled backwards as yet another wave came to break against the wall with a crash, and another. The whole sea was in turmoil, great black waves rearing out of it and storming towards the shore. There were no clouds in the sky yet, but the sea seemed to know they were on the way, and was rushing forwards and upwards to meet them.

Mr Panwallah had brought Hari to the Worli seaface to see the approach of the monsoon. He said he did this every year on a day in the first week of June. He had pulled down the shutters of his shop early, straightened the black cap on his head, asked Jagu to give Hari an evening off, and brought him here on the bus. He had also insisted on buying Hari a green coconut and a paper cone filled with puffed rice. Hari was shaking the cone into his hand and eating the puffed rice just like one of those lucky children brought here by their parents for an outing, enjoying themselves on the merry-go-rounds set up along the promenade and buying balloons and ice creams and coconuts. It made him feel one of them, a child again – not a small, shrivelled adult keeping up with the other adults in a hard world. The roaring wind off the sea with its salt tang, the sharp sting of spray from the waves and the sight of the great ocean stretching out all the way to Africa made him feel lighter and happier than he could remember feeling for a long time.

'Thank you, Mr Panwallah,' he remembered to say.

He did not know that evening how hard the monsoon made life for the people of Bombay.

On the tenth of June it came storming out of the sea and pouring on to the city just as Mr Panwallah had said it would. Like all the other citizens of Bombay, Hari stayed indoors and watched the rain like a great sheet being flung upon the city, and the water rising in the streets. The street in front of the eating house became first a gutter – all the rubbish of a year suddenly lifted up and carried away in a rush – and then a river. The drains became blocked, the rising tide forced the water up the big drain holes back into the streets, and they were flooded. Cars broke down and stalled in knee-deep greasy water.

For a while the urchins of the city had a wonderful time out in the rain, putting their shoulders to the cars and pushing them up to the higher reaches and earning some coins from the drivers. Hari and the two boys from the kitchen went out and made some pocket-money, too, and for the first time Hari saw his two fellow-cooks laughing as in drenched shirts and shorts, with wet faces and streaming hair, they demanded money from the drivers and heaved cars and taxis out of the first patches of waterlogging.

The city was washed clean not only of a year's dirt but also of the summer's heat, and the sudden dramatic drop in temperature gave everyone a lift: it was like a picnic, or a holiday. In fact it *was* a holiday for all the schoolchildren who could not get to school dry and therefore were not sent at all, and the office workers who could not get to work because buses and trains had stalled in the water that rose higher by the minute. 'Soon we'll need boats!' the urchins shouted as they splashed through the flood.

But it was not really a holiday for Hari and the two boys in the kitchen. Coolies and handcart pullers who could not get any work done came to sit in the Sri Krishna Eating House and asked for tea and hot meals. Jagu called in the boys from the street to get down to work. They worked overtime, without any break. The coal and the wood had all gone damp and it was difficult to get a fire started. When they did, it did not burn but smouldered and smoked, getting into their eyes and throats and making them cough and rub at their eyes with grimy hands. The customers brought mud into the eating room which had to be cleaned up constantly with a rag and a pail that soon seemed filled with mud. Sometimes they were made to go out and fetch cigarettes and then they were drenched and could not get dry but shivered miserably.

By evening Hari was more tired than he had ever been before, and it was still raining, pouring. He suddenly realized he would not be able to sleep in the park tonight – and perhaps not on any night during the monsoon.

When Jagu put out the light and took out the key to lock up the place for the night, Hari knew he could not go out into the rain and there was nothing to do but stretch out on the bench in the suffocating room and try to sleep. Of course he could not. That night he felt like a prisoner on his first night in jail.

It rained day and night, week after week. Even when the rain slowed from a downpour to a drizzle and the floods receded, nothing dried out, everything remained damp and muddy, and smelt. Every time Hari went out to empty the rubbish pail or to buy cigarettes for the customers, his shirt was soaked again and he spent the rest of the day with the wet cloth clinging to his body. He began to cough so badly that his chest hurt.

Mr Panwallah next door felt even worse and sniffed and coughed and wheezed without stop. One day he did not appear to pull the shutter up: he was sick. Hari had seen him red-eyed and feverish at the counter one day, leaving all the work to Hari because his head ached so badly, and the next day he did not come. Now Hari had no escape at all from the kitchen and the eating house, since he could go neither to the watch shop nor to the park. Locked up day and night in the Sri Krishna Eating House, he began to feel like a prisoner condemned to live in a prison cell.

Jagu must have sensed this. One night, when he was locking up the kitchen, he stopped to look at Hari, who would not lie down but sat on the floor, hugging his knees and coughing into his lap.

'You're ill,' he said. 'You had better come along with me. Come, I'll take you home.'

Hari was so grateful for the invitation to go anywhere that he got up and followed Jagu out of the shop and down the road without a word. He had no idea where Jagu lived or where he was being taken but he went: he was so grateful to be taken to someone's, anyone's house.

Jagu was the proprietor of a 'restaurant', the owner of an eating house on a busy street and had plenty of customers, yet his house was in a slum, one of those colonies of shacks made out of rags and flattened tin cans that are called *zopadpattis* in Bombay. There were not enough houses or flats in the city for the millions of people who came to work in it and earn a living in it, and since there were not enough, the rents of even the smallest flats were too high for people like Jagu. He counted himself lucky to be able to rent a shack in a *zopadpatti*.

These shacks clung to the side of a hill by the sea, on the other side of the wide boulevard to which Mr Panwallah had taken Hari to see the advancing monsoon. On the boulevard side of the hill the houses had been large and tall, pink and green and yellow, with names like Sunshine and Seagull, in which rich people lived. On the other side of the hill were the shacks of the poor, tumbling downhill into an open drain and a busy road.

As Hari followed Jagu along a narrow path, he felt his feet slipping in the soft mud. The whole hill seemed to be turning into mud. The shacks seemed to be coming loose and sliding into the choked gutter that separated the *zopadpatti* from the street.

Hari, wiping his nose with his shirt sleeve and pushing his hair out of his eyes, felt more and more worried as Jagu led him along the narrow path lined with these dismal shacks. Did Jagu really live in one of them? How could he bring Hari to such a place? He did, and he could, for he stopped in front of one of these structures of tin can, rag and plastic sheets, and pushed aside the rag that hung in the doorway, stooped and entered it. Then he beckoned to Hari to come in, and Hari too bent and crawled in.

All the rain and slush and mud from outside had crept in at the door and through the cracks in the walls and the ceiling as well. In fact, the mud floor was awash with rain water and the debris it brought along. Jagu's family was huddled on a string bed as if it were a raft. Their belongings, in tin and cardboard boxes, were perched on top of bricks and stones along the edges. Some bundles hung from the bamboo poles that acted as rafters.

Hari stood there helplessly, wondering whether he too was expected to clamber on to the string bed with the others. It was already crowded.

But no, there was a wooden bench which was not entirely covered with pots and pans and boxes and bundles. 'Sit here, Hari,' Jagu told him and then spoke to the family on the string bed. Several pairs of eyes peered at him from under the rags they held over their heads to keep off the rain from the leaking roof. It was very dark inside although there had been a faint glow outside from the streetlamps across the gutter.

Then a woman's voice began to speak. At first Hari could not understand what it said, it was so sharp and high-pitched and quick. After a while he heard curses that he knew and he began to feel even more worried and looked at Jagu for help.

'Be quiet,' Jagu growled. 'Get my dinner and bring an extra plate for the boy. He is ill. I am taking him to the dispensary for medicine tomorrow. He is going to sleep here tonight.'

The shrill, sharp voice went on and on and would not stop, although the bundles on the string bed did move and separate into individual figures. One of them stepped down into the mud and went and fetched food for the two of them on two tin plates.

'Hardly enough for us and you bring one more to be fed,' the woman screamed as she thrust the plates at them. 'So you'll get only half, that's what. You think I'll give your new friend my children's share? You think we can starve as long as you eat?'

'Quiet,' said Jagu fiercely, making a terrible face at her. 'Hold your tongue or I'll go out straight away to the toddy shop and have a drink there instead of this rotten food you prepare for me.'

'Go, go,' she screamed. 'As if I can stop you. That's all you want – to go to your toddy shop. All you want from me is an excuse. What do I care if you go and poison yourself? Go kill yourself with the poison the shops sell you – I will come and laugh at your funeral. I will take the children home to the village so we can starve in the fields and let the vultures pick our bones . . .'

Hari sat over his plate with his head sinking lower and lower, unwilling to eat a bite of the food. But Jagu had swallowed it all in great gulps and now got up saying, 'All right, if you force me – I'll go,' and disappeared, leaving Hari alone with the woman.

But as soon as he left, she fell silent. She huddled on the string bed, drew a rag over her head and stared at Hari from under it. He stared back. After a while she sniffed and started to pat the child who slept beside her. He heard her sigh heavily.

'Go, go to sleep,' she sighed, and Hari was not sure whether she spoke to him or to the child. 'What is there to do but to lie down and sleep? Or die? Men can go to the toddy shop and drink and forget, but we can do nothing, so we must lie down and sleep. Sleep,' she said again, patting the child and sighing.

Hari wanted to speak to her. He knew what made her speak in that bitter, sad tone. It was how Lila and he spoke to each other when they sat in their hut late at night, waiting for their father to come home from the village in the dark. Indeed, he felt as if this woman were speaking for him and for Lila and for their mother. He was no longer afraid of her.

'Does he drink every night?' he mumbled at last.

The woman shook her head. 'No. He is not as bad as some of the others in this *zopadpatti*. He does it only when he is very sad, or very worried.'

'My father drinks every night,' Hari told her. He had never said this to anyone before but now he found himself talking openly to this strange woman who had screamed at him and abused him for eating her food.

'He does, does he? And beats your mother? And starves you?' she asked, interested.

He nodded and coughed instead of speaking. He did not need to tell her – she already knew.

'Lie down, son. In the morning we'll get you medicine from the dispensary. The doctor there has medicine for coughs and colds. I take my baby to him, too. My baby is sick. She has fever,' and she began to pat the sleeping child at her side, sighing.

Hari curled up on the bench, tried to sleep and wondered why Jagu had brought him to this wretched home to add to his family's misery.

Next morning, while following Jagu along the path to the dispensary on the other side of the muddy hill – the rich and comfortable and happy side – Hari told him, 'I will go back to the shop, Jagu. There is no room for me here. I will go back.'

Jagu gave him a sharp look. 'Did that woman tell you to go? Don't listen to her – she's a devil, a she-devil.'

'No, she didn't say that,' Hari said quickly. 'But your child is sick, and she has enough to do. And the house –'

'Hmm,' said Jagu thoughtfully. 'The house is not at its best in the rain. In the dry season it is not so bad where we live. We have no water connection and she has to line up with all the other women at the pump to fetch water, but in the rainy season when there is water everywhere, it is even worse.' He nodded and Hari could see that he realized he had made a mistake in bringing Hari home. He had done it out of kindness and a wish to help, Hari knew, and he wanted to thank Jagu but could not.

At the dispensary, a broken building with a tin roof on which the rain drummed loudly, there was a long queue of men, women and children waiting on the veranda and out in the rain for the doctor to see to them. Seeing the queue, Jagu said gloomily, 'It will take a long time.'

Hari said, 'I will wait. Please go to the shop – I can wait alone.'

Jagu shuffled away, looking deeply ashamed for the muddle he had made of everything.

While Hari stood waiting, he saw Jagu's wife come up with the baby in her arms and an empty bottle for medicine in one hand, and stand right at the end of the queue, in the rain. Hari went to her and said, 'Let me get the medicine for you. Let me hold the baby.' She looked at him in surprise, then shook her head, saying, 'No, no – I can do that,' and he turned away, knowing he could not help her.

Hari stayed on at the eating house all through the monsoon for there was nowhere else in the city he could go. Mr Panwallah's shop next door remained shut and he was the only friend Hari had here. Once the watchman of the tall building who had first brought him to the Sri Krishna Eating House stopped by, under a big black umbrella, and called him out.

'How are you, boy?' he shouted to make himself heard above the spatter of raindrops. 'Still here? Working away? Liking it? Everything all right?'

Hari nodded and tried to smile. It was because of him that he had found shelter, a job, food and friends, and he knew he ought to be grateful although this was hard considering what the job, food and shelter were like. 'Yes, yes,' he said, 'all right,' because he knew it was better than what most people had in Bombay.

'You know what, boy? Those people you came to see that night at Seabird – they're back. They came back from abroad last week. Why don't you come and see them? They might have a job for you in their flat.'

Hari was taken aback: he had stopped thinking about them long ago. His time and his mind had become wholly occupied with his work in the kitchen and with the watchmending he was learning from Mr Panwallah and with saving money to take home: he had no time in which to think of the future beyond the next day and the next. Now his head filled with thoughts of that first night in Bombay, how amazed he had been by the lights, the great buildings, the crowds. He thought of the block of flats, the lift that had taken him up as if by magic, the polished door that opened on to that shining room, and the haughty servant in the white clothes. He kept thinking about them as he went back to kneading dough, scrubbing pans, rolling out *chapatis* and serving lentils or tea. Could he leave all this behind and go? Could he find himself a place in that rich, gleaming world of high-rise apartments, take part in that fairytale world of servants, cars, holidays, money and freedom?

It made him feel feverish to think about it. He could not go to sleep that night, wondering if he should take the watchman's advice and try his luck there the next time he had a free afternoon.

That night a great storm broke over the Indian Ocean and lashed the city. It began with daggers of lightning striking through the black clouds banked in the sky, and peals of thunder that echoed from one building to another. Early in the morning before daylight, it began to pour with rain. Once again the streets were flooded. The wind blew up from the sea and hurled the rain at the walls and windows of the city. One of the great trees in the park came down with a crash and lay across one of the lanes, blocking the traffic which piled up, madly hooting and honking. There was chaos on the streets. Of course buses and cars broke down and stalled everywhere. Hari watched from the eating house door, shivering in his damp clothes.

They had few customers that day – even pedestrians were keeping off the streets. One lorry driver who came in for tea had to stay all day, his lorry stranded in hub-deep water. He had a transistor radio with him which he put on the table beside his tea tumbler and listened to while he ate and drank. The boys hung around, listening. They listened to the songs from the Bombay cinema, they listened to advertisement jingles about toothpaste, cleaning powder, cooking oil and face cream. They listened to a play about kings, queens and battles lost and won. Then, at the end of the play when the king had died and the queen had sung her last song, the voice of the announcer broke in with the news.

The news was all about the storm: how it had rained ten inches in twelve hours, how the whole city was 'paralysed'. Then the announcer went on to say: 'Ten fishing boats are reported lost at sea. Many fishermen are feared dead.'

Hari gave a cry and put his ear to the radio. 'Where?' he shouted, as if demanding an answer from the announcer. 'Where?'

The boys began to laugh at him and the lorry driver grinned, but Hari got his answer.

'Search parties are to be sent out from Alibagh as soon as the storm subsides.'

'Alibagh!' cried Hari, staring at the three watching faces. 'That's my home! That's my land!'

'All right, boy, all right,' said the lorry driver, a Sikh with big moustaches and a red turban. 'You're not a fisherman, are you? You're not on a boat. You're safe and sound in a restaurant with plenty of good food and hot tea. Don't get so upset.'

Jagu was more understanding. He had hardly spoken to Hari since the dismal failure of his visit to their house, but now he grunted, 'What's the matter? Is your father a fisherman? Does he own one of those boats?'

'No,' said Hari, shaking his head, 'no,' and went into the kitchen to worry by himself It was true that his father was not in one of those boats, and that his family owned none. But it was the men from his village who went out fishing, and it could be men he knew, friends or neighbours, who were lost. He suddenly remembered Biju's boat and thought that by now it must be launched and on the high seas.

He thought of the sails one saw along the horizon, and the lights of the boats by night which were visible from the beach. He thought of the catch coming in in the evenings, the voices of the women quarrelling over the baskets of shining fish on the sand. He thought of his net and how he walked through the shallows with it. He thought of the crows picking up the crabs he caught, and the gulls swooping low over the waves in search of fish. He thought of the heron standing stock still on a stone by the pond near their hut, and the blue flash of the kingfisher as it darted from the trees. He thought of Lila coming down the path with a basket of flowers to sprinkle on the rock in the sea, and of Bela and Kamal sitting on the rocks and chipping at the limpets. He thought he heard Pinto bark. How he longed for them all. Sitting down on his heels by the fire, he put his head on his knees, shut his eyes and tried hard to see them again – beautiful and bright, his own.

When the monsoon came, the girls hastily stitched together palm leaves to cover the old, ragged, thatch roof, and more to cover the doors and windows of the big house, an extra protection against the rain that swept in from the sea and beat upon the beach and the huts night and day without stopping or slowing. The great dark monsoon clouds seemed to well out of the sea into the sky and the great waves surged wildly up to meet them, blending in one massive sheet of water that hung everywhere, on earth and in the sky.

The fishing boats were drawn up the creek that swelled with the high monsoon tides, making the boats rock and crash into each other, their sails and banners all taken down and put away so that the masts were bare against the sky. The villagers stayed in their huts as far as possible, venturing out under big black umbrellas only when they had to. The ponds and creeks filled, the fields were flooded and slushy, weeds spread rampant and frogs croaked madly through the night. Fires were smoky and the huts were damp and gloomy, the rain beating down on the thatch and leaking on to the mud floors, making everything so wet that it didn't seem possible they would ever be dry again.

With the fishermen idle, unable to go to sea in such storms, there was no fish to be had. Even the men sat plaiting ropes and thatching palm leaves, occupations usually left to the women. Probably they drank even more toddy than at any other time of year, but Lila's father had given up drinking.

He sat outside the hospital, keeping an eye on the comings and goings of the nurses and doctors, and made sure his wife had all she needed. He smoked a small hand-held clay hookah and sat hunched on the veranda, watching the rain stream down. Lila still came loyally once a week, bringing him some of the money she had earned at *Mon Repos* so he could buy himself tobacco and tea and snacks. It was worth struggling through the rain and coming on the wet, muddy bus just to see him so sober and quiet and her mother better and brighter than she had been the week before. These visits were always very happy ones even though they all cried when they parted.

Sometimes the girls went together to the village to buy provisions. They had to wait till the rain slackened. The whole village looked shut and empty with everyone indoors.

But the fishermen could not afford to stay indoors for the three months of the monsoon. As their stocks of grain dwindled and their meals grew fewer and smaller, their families looked pinched and hollow-cheeked. When the rain slowed down, they would go out on the beach, climb into their boats, stare at the sky and mutter to each other about the weather.

One day, when there was a lull in the rain, the heavy grey clouds lay still along the horizon and did not appear to be drawing any closer, a party of fishermen set out in their boats. Lila was coming back from the village shop with a bag of grain and saw the boats wildly tossing on the waves, their sails flapping and creaking loudly and the men hurling themselves from one side to the other in order to keep the boats steady. Old Biju, who would not risk his fine new boat at sea in this season, stood at the mouth of the creek, shouting at them.

'Fools, come back! Your boats aren't built for this weather.'

'The weather is fine, can't you see?' one of the men shouted back. 'We've had enough of sitting at home like old women.'

'You'll be drowned,' Biju roared after the men, 'and your boats wrecked,' but they only laughed, thrilled at being out at sea again.

Lila did not stop to watch any more, the sight of the small boats bucking on the waves alarmed her and she felt uneasy. She had not been home long when she heard an ominous rumble of thunder. All night lightning flashed and thunder boomed while the coconut trees creaked and swung dangerously over their hut. The sounds of the wind and the sea were so loud that the girls hid under their cotton blankets, saying their ears ached, not admitting that they did it out of fear.

Early that morning the greatest storm of that monsoon broke. At times it seemed that their hut would be blown to splinters. Lila feared that one of the coconut trees would fall upon their roof. The water in the creek rose minute by minute, turning what had been a marsh into a lake. Bela and Kamal were beside themselves with excitement, but Lila grew quieter and quieter – she had seen the boats out at sea but she had not told them about that.

It was three days before the storm lessened and another two before the clouds parted and let through a little pale, watery sunlight. The three girls ran down to the beach to see if they could reach the rocks and offer a basket of flowers and kum-kum powder. They were standing in the waves, screaming as they grew wetter and wetter, when old Hira-*bai* from the hut behind theirs came by on her way back from the village and stopped to tell them of the great drama of the fishing boats. The little girls were horrified, and Lila was eager to hear the details.

The boats had been lost for nearly four days. When the storm began to withdraw, a search party organized by the navy and the coastguards at Alibagh set out. Biju had insisted on accompanying them and was soon at their helm. It was he who had spotted what remained of the fishing fleet: three boats had sunk, the rest were battered and broken. Three fishermen had drowned. They rescued the rest and brought them back, starved and feverish and ill.

The men from the navy and the coastguards had praised Biju and thanked him but the fishermen had been too tired to say a word and had gone limping home.

'I told them – I told them not to go: the weather was too treacherous for those little matchstick boats,' Biju roared, standing by the creek and supervising the anchoring and tying up of their boats. This was a great day for him, the day when the prowess of his own superior boat had been proved for all to see. He was only sorry these thick-headed fishermen refused to admit it. 'Admit it – you'll have to admit it,' he roared. 'You have to have a boat with a diesel engine for this weather – your sails will only help to drown you.'

A few of the fishermen's wives were still standing on the sand, watching and listening. One of them muttered, 'Yes, yes, Biju, but who can afford boats like yours?'

'Ours may be weak and useless, yes,' another agreed, 'but still – we have to eat and our men must fish.'

Biju glared, his boasting and bragging cut short. 'One day everyone will have to build boats like mine,' he growled at them. 'Things have to change. Then they will improve. Yes,' he shouted as they retreated. 'Improve! Change!' and stalking down the muddy bank of the creek he went to see to his own boat before leaving it to the wind and rain that had already started up again and was beginning to drum upon the wooden decks and cut rivulets through the wet sand.

Suddenly he recognized a figure amongst the knot of people still standing on the bank, watching. 'You,' he shouted, pointing at him with a thick, ringed finger. 'You there. Now do you see what a fine boat I have?' and he roared with laughter because the man who was trying to hurry away without an answer was the watchman from the factory site who had made fun of his boat when it was being built. He had learnt better now – the villagers, their boats, their crafts were not quite so sorry as he had said they were. Of course he hated to admit it and was hurrying back to the shelter of his hut.

'Yes,' Hira-*bai* chuckled as she described it all to the girls. – 'It was Biju's proudest day all right.'

'Yes,' said Lila, 'but how must the other men and their wives have felt?'

Hira-*bai* lifted her hand to the sky. 'Just as they have always felt, my dear.' She sighed. 'Leave it to the gods – that is all we can do, leave it to the gods,' and she turned and went slowly up the beach to the line of coconut palms.

Lila, Bela and Kamal, huddled around the damp, smoking fire in their hut that night, were grateful that they could eat because of the money paid them by the gentleman in the house who was not driven away by the monsoon but stayed on and walked about in it as if he didn't notice it at all. They were grateful for his mere presence, too, in the absence of both their father and brother. Listening to the storms outside, they wondered about Hari. Why did Hari not come?

He had sent them one postcard to say he was in Bombay, safe, but why did he not return? They sat in silence, listening to the frogs clamouring in the dark and the rain sliding off the palm leaves on to their roof and dripping.

Finally, 'When do you think Hari will come?' sighed Bela, drawing lines on the mud floor with her finger.

'He can't come now – the ferry will have stopped for the monsoon,' said Lila, trying to sound sensible and brisk. 'Perhaps he will come when the monsoon is over. Perhaps he will come at Diwali.'

11

'YOU'LL go back one day, boy, don't you worry,' Mr Panwallah said kindly. 'You've not come so far away – you can go back.'

'When?' said Hari wildly. 'I want to go now.'

'Wait till the rains are over, boy. The ferry doesn't travel to Rewas in the rainy season. When the rains are over, you can take the ferry and go back. You'll have more money saved up by then, won't you? And I'm getting stronger, I'll soon be back at the shop to teach you more about watchmending. Once you start mending watches on your own, you can collect the payment, it will be yours, not mine. Does that sound good? Eh? Then you can go back and set up as the village watchmender.'

Hari laughed at the old man's ignorance. What watches and clocks were there in his village where everyone told the time by the sun? Old Biju might have a clock but it would have rusted in the salt air, he knew, and be as useless as his television set. Still, he felt happy at the thought and was grateful to Mr Panwallah for giving it to him.

It was Mr Panwallah he had come running to see when he could not bear his longing for home any more, Mr Panwallah he had searched out and told about the lost fishing fleet. The old man had not been to the shop since he fell ill. The shutter had been drawn down ever since. But one day a customer came looking for his watch and asked Jagu next door if he knew what had happened to the old watchmender and to the watches he was supposed to be mending. Hari overheard Jagu giving him Mr Panwallah's address.

'What?' he cried, dropping a duster on to the floor. 'Where does he live?' It had not occurred to him that Jagu would know.

Jagu repeated the address and Hari immediately begged to be given an hour off so that he could go and visit the old man. It was not far from the shop; it was right beside the Grant Road station at the end of the road and Hari found it quite easily. Quickly he climbed the rickety wooden staircase, past the sweet shop at street level, past the small clinic for birds and animals on the first floor, past doors with withered garlands of marigolds hanging over them and rice powder designs drawn on their thresholds to the top floor where Mr Panwallah had a tiny room and a balcony full of plants in old tins and boxes.

Here he sat on a broken cane chair, looking very white and frail – but alive and improving. He had had 'flu to begin with but it had grown worse and turned into bronchitis. His neighbours were afraid he would have to be taken to hospital but he looked so weak that they decided to let him stay in his own bed and took turns at bringing him meals and hot drinks. The doctor who lived in the flat below his had treated him free – they had been neighbours for more than fifty years: Mr Panwallah was popular in that block, much loved and even, it now was clear, much cherished. They had all been relieved when he recovered but insisted he stay at home and rest till the rainy weather was over so that he would not get wet while going to work and fall ill again. He had been delighted when Hari had burst in upon him. He had been sitting quietly, gazing out over the sheets of corrugated iron that roofed the railway station at the pigeons that sat on it and flew up in flocks through the columns of gritty smoke every time a train came roaring in or went screeching out.

Hari found himself sitting on a stool at his feet, drinking very sweet tea from a tumbler brought up from the tea stall by an urchin who had fed and helped to look after Mr Panwallah all through his illness: there was more than one boy who was grateful to Mr Panwallah for help given at one time or another. Hari sat sipping tea and telling him all about Thul. Mr Panwallah listened with his head cocked to one side like a wise old bird, and all the time he stroked and petted the grey cat that slept curled upon his lap.

'Yes,' he nodded, 'soon it will be Coconut Day, the end of the monsoon when everyone offers coconuts to the sea and the boats can safely set out again. Then you can catch your ferry home. You should never have left, boy. You shouldn't have left your mother and sisters to come here. Look how thin and sick you have grown here – tchh!'

'There was nothing left for me to do there,' Hari explained. 'My father sold our fishing boat long ago. He sold our cow, too. I had no work – just a small plot of land to grow vegetables in, too small. And now a big factory is going to come up in Thul, and they will take up all our land and it is said there will be no fishing or farming left to do. I had to come to Bombay to find work.'

'You can find work anywhere,' piped Mr Panwallah, sitting up very straight and fixing his bird-like eyes on Hari. 'As long as you can use your hands,' he said, lifting up his ten spindly fingers and waggling them, 'you can find work for them. And you have to be willing to learn – and to change – and to grow. If they take away your land you will have to learn to work in their factory instead. If you can't stop it, you must learn to use it – don't be afraid!'

'Our elders say only engineers with degrees from colleges will get work there. They will not need fishermen or farmers. We will not get work.'

'Hmm,' said Mr Panwallah and chewed his lip for a while. 'Yes, perhaps. But there will be other work, besides the factory. You can get work as a builder, or a roadmaker, when they are at a building stage. Later, the engineers and mechanics will come to live there in the new housing colonies and they will need people to work for them. They will need food, too – vegetables and milk and fruit and eggs. You will find you can sell the vegetables you grow, and the coconuts. Perhaps you will be able to buy a cow or chickens and make a living from them. Yes, yes, yes – think about it, Hari, there will be plenty of work. They will even bring watches and clocks with them for you to repair,' he laughed, showing his pink, toothless gums. 'So your watchmending skills won't be useless after all! Perhaps one day you will own the first watch repair shop in Thul – what do you say to that?'

Hari laughed back in surprise. Why had he never thought of that himself?

'Oh, Mr Panwallah,' he cried, 'when will you come back to the shop and teach me more?'

'Yes, yes, yes.' Mr Panwallah laughed, petting his old grey cat with quick little pats. 'I will come and I will teach you – wait for me, don't run away so soon, boy.'

'I won't,' Hari promised. 'I want to learn more.'

'Good!' cried Mr Panwallah. 'That's what I wanted to hear you say. Learn, learn, learn – so that you can grow and change. Things change all the time, boy – nothing remains the same. When our earth was covered with water, all creatures lived in it and swam. When the water subsided and land appeared, the sea creatures crawled out and learned to breathe and walk on land. When plants grew into trees, they learned to climb them. When there were not enough plants left to eat, they learned to hunt and kill for food. Don't think that is how things have remained. No, boy, they are still changing – they will go on changing – and if you want to survive, you will have to change too. The wheel turns and turns and turns: it never stops and stands still. Look, even Bombay is not always the same. Fifty years ago there were hills, gardens, beautiful palaces and villas where you now see slums, shops, traffic, crowds. Once I lived in a villa with a garden and roses and fountains – now I live in a pigeon roost over a railway station!' He cackled with laughter as though it were all a great joke. 'So Hari the fisherman, Hari the farmer will have to become Hari the poultry farmer or Hari the watchmender!'

Hari beamed to see Mr Panwallah so excited and lively. If he was so much better, he would surely come back to the shop soon and start teaching Hari again. Hari knew he still had much to learn.

'You are lucky,' Mr Panwallah twinkled at him, sinking back into his chair. 'You are young. You can change and learn and grow. Old people can't, but you can. I know you will.'

And so the wheel turned again, just as Mr Panwallah had said it would, and things got better just as earlier they had got worse. The rain slowed to a drizzle. Mr Panwallah came back to open his shop, looking very pale and fragile but full of eagerness to take up work again: he had so much work piled up that Hari had to spend more time helping him and less and less time in the eating house.

Jagu did not seem to mind. He did not seem to want to see so much of Hari or talk to him after that visit to his house that had proved so unfortunate. Perhaps he was sorry Hari had met his wife and family and seen how they lived. It made him look away from Hari and simply nod or grunt when Hari asked for permission to spend a few hours at Mr Panwallah's.

Hari did not, after all, go up the hill to the tall block of flats where the de Silvas lived. He felt he could not bear the shame and humiliation of finding his way into it and asking for work. He was no longer the frightened, confused boy who crawled into any hole where he could find shelter and protection. He knew he could make choices and decisions now. He did not really wish to live in a rich man's house as a servant. He felt he would only make a fool of himself, break the glass and china, leave dirty finger and footprints on shining surfaces, show his ignorance over such things as lifts, doorbells, telephones and cars. He was not a city boy and he did not want to become one. Ever since he had heard the news on the radio of the fishing boats lost at sea and felt as disturbed as if his own boats were lost, or his own father and brothers, he had known that he belonged to Thul and that he would go back. It was wonderful to be able to choose what you wanted to do in life, and choose he would.

'I will go back after the rains are over,' he told Jagu. 'I had better tell you now in case you want to find someone to take my place.'

Jagu only nodded and looked away. 'When?' he mumbled.

'After Coconut Day,' said Hari. 'Some time after Coconut Day.'

'Stay till Diwali,' Jagu muttered, looking down at the dirty table-top and drumming on it nervously. 'Then my brother will come from my village to help me. Till then, stay.'

Hari wanted to refuse: he had not planned to stay so long, but he could not protest. Jagu had been so good to him, had given him food and shelter and saved his life, even tried to make him one of his family although that had not been so successful: he could not refuse. He quietly picked up the dirty plates from the table and took them away to wash.

'Jagu won't let me go till Diwali,' he told Mr Panwallah unhappily.

'No?' cried Mr Panwallah. 'Oh, don't look so gloomy, boy. Diwali will be here before you know it. Look up at the sky – the clouds are rolling away, Coconut Day will be here soon! And then it will be Diwali next. So many festivals, one after the other. I think it is a good idea – to go home at Diwali, the best day in the whole year. Till then, you can stay here and learn – I have so much to teach you still. You did that watch I gave you yesterday perfectly: when the owner comes to fetch it, I will make him pay *you* for it. But there is more to learn. Look at this watch that has come from Japan. Electronic. See, in my old age I have to learn about a new kind of watch. You can learn, too. Sit down. Wipe your hands. I am going to open it now – look –' and they both peered into the mysterious insides of the watch, studying its tiny parts that worked so perfectly.

While they worked, Hari said, 'Mr Panwallah, you celebrate Coconut Day and Diwali and yet you are not a Hindu, are you? I thought you are a Parsee and celebrate only the Parsee festivals.'

'Oh no, no, no, boy,' cried Mr Panwallah comically. 'What would be the fun of that? And why should I miss the fun of all the Hindu and Muslim festivals? No, no, I believe in sharing everything, enjoying everything. That is why I have so much fun, eh? No gloom for me, eh?'

They were still happily working at the Japanese watch when the owner of the Rolex that Hari had repaired came along for it and Mr Panwallah told him to pay Hari and not him. The man looked a bit puzzled but handed over a ten rupee note to Hari at Mr Panwallah's request. Hari stood staring at the note: he suddenly felt he was not a child any longer, that he was a man. So when Mr Panwallah cried, 'Well, aren't you pleased? Won't you smile?' he could not. He nodded and put the money away in his pocket very carefully.

'Before I go home, I will buy presents for my sisters,' he said. 'I will save all my watch money for that.'

Coconut Day came at last, even before the rains were properly over. It no longer poured day and night as during the monsoon – only drizzled occasionally from a passing cloud. The clouds were no longer a mass of grey wool blanketing the city but had separated into creamy puffs that floated along in the sunshine and the breeze. The sea was much calmer: the waves no longer towered over the boulevards and crashed across the streets but simply heaved, muddy and tired after all the storms. The buildings of the city were still damp and mouldy but no longer stood in several feet of water and were beginning to dry.

On Coconut Day it drizzled in the morning but that was when people were still indoors, doing *puja* with sticks of incense and garlands of marigolds and dishes of sweets that were placed before Ganesha, the elephant-headed god who was the patron god of Bombay. When the crowds came pouring out on to the streets in the afternoon, carrying coconuts to throw into the sea, the sun had come out and gilded the battered, untidy city with a sheen of gold.

Hari and Mr Panwallah were among the thousands and thousands of people who streamed down to Chowpatty, the beach Hari had taken for a fairground when he saw it on his first day in Bombay. Today it really *was* a fairground. The police were out, directing the traffic, making way for the processions to cross Marine Drive on to the beach – again reminding Hari of that first day in Bombay. Every inch of sand was covered: there were more hawkers and stall-keepers than ever, selling hot salted snacks, ice creams, coloured drinks, balloons, tin whistles and paper horns to excited children. And, of course, green coconuts. Everyone bought a green coconut to carry into the sea as an offering to it at the end of the season of storms, in thanksgiving for its safe end.

Mr Panwallah, still rather white and bent from his long illness but very cheerful and almost energetic again, bought Hari a coconut. 'You keep your money for presents for the family,' he said when Hari tried to pay for it – and they pushed their way through the crowds to the edge of the sea. There were men pounding on drums that hung by straps from their necks, and others who danced behind and before them, sticking out their elbows and bending their knees and shouting as they frolicked along. Women were dressed in their brightest and newest saris – pink and yellow, violet and orange – and all had flowers in their hair. Some of them threw red powder into the air and it settled on their heads and shoulders and glinted in the afternoon sun.

Then they were out on the flat, wet sand for the tide was out, far out. The wet sand glistened and reflected the great pink clouds that sailed along in the golden sky. Children were running barefoot over it to the sea where fishermen waited in boats for those who wanted to row out to sea and immerse their coconuts in the deep. Others were just tossing their coconuts in or wading in to set them afloat. Thousands of coconuts bobbed and floated and sank. Hundreds of urchins splashed through the waves and dived for them.

Suddenly Hari pushed aside the two boys on either side of him, dashed past a tall man in front of him, and to Mr Panwallah's astonishment, shouted, 'It's mine! It's mine!' and dived into the spray to grab a coconut thrown by someone else and fiercely fought over by three or four other boys. Hari was waist-deep in water, the spray was being churned up all around him, and there he stood, clutching the coconut to him and beaming triumphantly at Mr Panwallah.

Mr Panwallah laughed with amazement. As Hari came out dripping with his prize, he chuckled. 'So, you've become a real city boy at last, have you? You've learned to push and fight your way with the city boys, have you? Hari, Hari – I never thought I would see you do such a thing.'

Hari began to feel ashamed and looked around for a beggar to whom he could give the coconut, but Mr Panwallah was not shocked: he was laughing.

'Yes, you can manage now,' he said, in a pleased way. 'You will manage all right – I can see I don't have to worry about you any more.'

I2

HARI came back to Thul not by ferry after all but by bus – Jagu and Mr Panwallah having bought him a ticket jointly for the bus. Mr Panwallah had said goodbye to him at the shop door, quietly slipping him another ten rupee note as a farewell present, and sniffing to keep back his tears, while Jagu had taken the morning off from work to accompany him to the bus depot and see him on to the right bus. 'Got your money safe with you, Hari?' he kept asking anxiously. 'Be careful of pickpockets. Don't touch your pocket, don't let anyone see you have so much money with you ...' for he was as anxious as Hari himself that his earnings got to the family in Thul safely. Again and again Hari had to promise to be careful, to send a postcard as soon as he reached Thul, to keep in touch with Jagu. Then at last the bus drew out and there was nothing to do but wave to each other silently.

As he left the city behind him – the slums, the peeling grey houses, the open foul-smelling gutters, the wayside bazaars, bus depots and traffic – he pressed his face to the window, searching for signs of the open country. They crossed a long, broad bridge and below it was the sea – not the sea as he knew it at Thul but the sea that separated Bombay from the mainland, a marshy sea that sank and swelled with the tide. Still, it smelt of salt as well as of mud and there were not only clumps of reeds at the edges but fishing boats and nets and glittering piles of 'windowpane' oysters as well. Hari shook with excitement but after that there was another long dreary stretch – the factory belt of Thana, pouring out evil-smelling smoke and chemicals into the discoloured sky, all the land around blighted and bare, not a blade of grass to be seen and the few remaining trees coated with suffocating dust. Hari wondered if this could possibly be the way that the green coastline from Rewas to Alibagh would look like one day.

There were a few signs of the beginnings of such a transformation: the highway was being widened, a railway bridge under construction, old large trees cut down and bulldozers and steamrollers at work, but the rice still stood golden and ripe in the fields, the low hills beyond them were violet and bronze, the sky clear and blue. They crossed a flat and lazy river that wound through the rice fields, then drove through a forest of large-leafed *sal* trees and at last were out on the coastline and Hari could see the coconut palms once more and the blur of blue in the distance that was the sea.

The bus set him down on the highway beside the hill with the temple on top. Although the old dusty road was being widened and tarred and many of the *sal* and banyan trees along it had been cut down to clear the way, Thul itself seemed unchanged. The hill stood, sunlit and sere, and it was still topped by the small white cube of the temple. Hari turned off the highway into the dusty, deeply rutted path between the coconut and betel palms that wound through the silent, sleepy village.

Hari came down the path through the coconut grove to the cluster of old gnarled casuarina trees on the beach. Here the breeze blew up salt and fresh, and there was the sea. The real sea, the open sea, not the sea that lapped the island of Bombay. Hari sank down on the roots of a casuarina, cupped his chin in his hand and stared and stared and stared at it. He wanted to make sure it was exactly as he remembered it, and it was. The tide was coming in, it boomed and thundered on the silver sand. The three black rocks were being submerged, only the tops showed above the creamy froth on the waves. Out along the horizon the sails of the fishing fleet showed like the wings of gulls or like butterflies, white and bright and brave against the skyline. Closer to shore were the two small islands of Undheri and Kundheri, rocky and green. Smaller fishing craft bobbed around them, trying to get back to land, to the village.

Sighing with relief, Hari got up and turned into the path over the dunes that were webbed with seaside morning glory, their flowers unfurled in flat mauve saucers. He passed his single small field and saw that the girls had sown the usual crop of *tindli* in it – the tiny marrows hung from the grapelike vines that had been trained over a bamboo trellis. He passed the white bungalow, *Mon Repos,* and noticed that its monsoon wrapping of thatch had been removed and that it gleamed white in the greenery. Then he came to the creek where the heron still stood on its stone, fishing, the kingfisher dived down in a flash of blue and the egret rose up from the reeds as white as snow. He crossed the log that lay across the creek and saw that the frangipani tree was in flower. In its shade the old hut looked as dark and dismal as ever, its earthen walls crumbling, its palm-leaf thatch hanging crooked and tattered over the eaves.

He would change it all: he would rebuild the hut, he would work on it now that he was home and make it bright and cheerful and happy.

'Lila, Bela, Kamal!' he called.

In an instant Lila was at the door, her old purple sari gathered about her, her face peeping out, brown and curious. When she saw him, she gasped. They stared at each other. Then she ran out crying, 'Hari! Hari, I knew you would come. It's Diwali tomorrow and I knew you'd come!'

'How did you know? I didn't write.'

'Oh, I knew, I knew you would,' Lila smiled. 'And we made sweets for you, Hari – come and eat.'

Hari wanted to ask a hundred questions, all at once, about their mother, their father, Bela and Kamal, about the village and Biju's boat and everything. Instead, he followed Lila into the house. Old and shabby it might be, but how shady and cool it was. He felt grateful for it, just as it was, and stood breathing in its air silently. Only the invisible pigeons could be heard, letting flow their musical notes like soft, feathered bubbles trickling through the air.

Then Lila came towards him with a brass tray on the palm of her hand. It was heaped with the sweets she had made of rice powder and cream, sugar and flour and semolina and coconut.

Hari said, 'But I must wash first: I am dusty.' He went out by the back door where the big earthenware jar stood filled with water from the well and tipping it over, he washed his face and hands, sprinkling some of the cool water on his hair as well. He felt that in all the nine months that he had spent in Bombay he had not had a wash as cool and refreshing as this.

When he turned Lila was standing in the doorway with a towel and he took it from her and wiped himself.

'How good the water feels here,' he said.

'Our well is sweet, you know,' she said, smiling.

'But so sweet – I had forgotten.' He shook his head, making drops fly. 'I forgot too much. Lila, where's Mother?' He did not dare look at her face for fear there would be a sign on it of bad news, but Lila looked back at him steadily.

'Mother is away in hospital, in Alibagh. The de Silvas took her there in the car. I go to see her sometimes, when I have the bus fare. She is much better.'

'How –?'

'With good food and proper medicine, I suppose. The doctor said it was anaemia which she got because of having poor food to eat.'

Hari tried hard to take that in. He knew the food they ate was inadequate but he had not known you could fall ill because of that. Now he would have to see to it that they ate better.

'I have all sorts of plans, Lila,' he burst out. 'I'll tell you –'

'Come, eat your sweets first. We made them for Diwali but we'll start celebrating today,' she laughed and went to get the tray with the sweets. Hari reached out for his favourite, a fried dumpling stuffed with sweet semolina and grated coconut, and bit into it greedily. It was crisp and delicate, the way Lila always made them. His mouth was still full when Bela and Kamal arrived.

They didn't know what to do next – hug each other, talk or eat sweets. They tried to do everything at once, and there was hubbub. Then Hari brought out presents for them – the presents Mr Panwallah had helped him purchase in Bombay with his watch repair money – bangles for the younger girls, metal ones with a gold and silver wash that made them shine, and a sari for Lila: not one of those thick homespun ones one could buy in the village, but a mill-made one of filmy, silky cloth, striped pink and white like some freshly bloomed morning flower. The three girls were wonder-struck when he unfolded it for them to see – nothing so pretty, so expensive or so fashionable had ever come into their house before. Lila gasped and the little girls squealed and pressed their hands to their mouths.

'Hari-*bhai*, where did you get so much money from? How could you spend so much?'

'I've brought back money, too,' he assured them. 'I saved up everything I earned in Bombay, I never spent anything there – I never went to the cinema or even bought a cigarette. I had two jobs,' he boasted – he could not help it, he knew the girls were enjoying it as much as he. 'I worked in an eating house where the proprietor gave me free board and lodging, as well as a salary, and I worked in a watchmender's shop next door. I was paid for the watches I mended – I have learned to repair watches, you know.'

'Repair watches?' cried Bela and Kamal in amazement.

'Repair watches?' echoed Lila hollowly, her face falling. It seemed the most useless skill anyone could bring back to the fishing village of Thul where no man ever had need to look at a watch in order to know when to take his boat out or when to bring back the fish. The tide told you that, and the sun.

Hari could tell she was disappointed. 'I know there are no watches here now, Lila – but wait till the factory comes up, and the housing colony is built. Then there will be plenty of people with watches around here – and I'll be the only man in Thul who knows how to oil and repair them so that they won't have to go all the way to Bombay to get it done. Things will change here, Lila.'

'Will they?' she asked doubtfully. 'When? How long will it take? And what are we to do till then?'

'But I've brought back money with me, too. I want to discuss that with you – and with Mother when I go to see her.' He did not mention their father – he knew that would be useless. 'We can put it to some use. I thought we might buy chickens and start a poultry farm in our field: it is too small for a market garden but it is big enough for a poultry farm. We could begin by selling eggs in the village. By the time the factory comes up and all those workers come to live here, we shall have chickens to sell, too. We can make a living with a poultry farm.'

Bela and Kamal shouted with delight. They thought it a wonderful idea. They passed the tray of sweets round once more.

'You two can look after the chickens when I set up my watch shop,' Hari told them. 'I'll get the poultry farm started and then hand it over to you to run.' He beamed at them because he could see they liked the idea.

'It will be the first poultry farm in Thul,' Kamal shouted. 'There is one at Kihim, and several in Alibagh, but this will be the first one in Thul – and it will be ours.'

'There used to be one here,' Lila reminded them. 'Old Sabu had one – you can still see all the broken pens and the wire netting in his garden. It failed.'

'That's because there was no one in Thul to buy his eggs and chickens, Lila,' Hari explained. 'And he had no van in which he could take them to Bombay to sell. But now people will be coming to Thul instead – thousands of them – we'll have more buyers then we can supply. You'll see, Lila – it'll flourish; it can't fail. And there'll be eggs and chicken for Mother to eat, too,' he added, trying hard to coax her into being cheerful.

She smiled at once at the thought. 'It'll be good for Mother,' she agreed. 'She might even be able to help – when she's stronger.'

'You'll have to tell me everything. Give me all the news. You never wrote.'

'We didn't know where you were. Whenever anyone went to Bombay, we sent messages, but no one could find you.'

He nodded. 'I wanted to be by myself for a while, on my own. Father –' and at last he said the word he did not want to say – 'Father, where is he?'

It was evident from the loudness and cheerfulness of his sisters' voices that their father was not inside, sleeping his usual drunken daytime sleep.

'He's in Alibagh,' Lila told him quietly. 'He followed Mother. When the de Silvas took her away, he was wild. Very angry. He screamed and shouted and broke all our water pots. He was drunk, you see. But he stopped drinking and followed her to Alibagh to see that she was properly looked after. He has stayed there ever since, he never came back. When I go to see her, I always find him sitting on the veranda outside her room or sometimes out in the hospital compound. He says she may need him so he stays where she can call him.'

'Is he drinking there?'

She shook her head. 'I don't think so. He seems to have stopped. He hasn't money for it, you see. The de Silvas gave him some and I take him a little – enough for food, not for toddy. He hasn't asked for more. I don't think he wants to drink any more.'

'And those Khanekar men – have they come around again?'

'No, they've left us alone,' Lila breathed gratefully. 'I think they do feel bad after all about Pinto.'

They all sat in silence, thinking about Pinto, about their father, about this strange new turn in their lives. Then Lila got up, saying, 'Hari, let's go to the beach and buy some fish for your homecoming dinner. Let's all go. Then you can tell us everything as we go.'

But when they went out on the beach and found the whole sky alight with sunset's glow and the wet ridged sand of the beach reflecting its pink and rose and violet hues, Hari could not speak for delight. He ran on to the wet sand, feeling it under his bare feet with joy. Bela and Kamal chased him. He dodged them. Lila laughed. Hari threw back his head and whooped so that the gulls rose from the sea's edge and wheeled about in the sky, mewing. He felt like a new person, like someone who had emerged from a tightly shut box and now saw the light and felt the breeze for the first time. He could have been newly born – a butterfly emerged from a cocoon. Bela caught one arm of his and Kamal caught the other.

Laughing, they walked down the beach, watching the gulls as they swooped low to pick up the long, eel-like fish that the village women dried on the clay flats and hung from bamboo trellises in the sun. One gull flew up with one of these 'Bombay duck' – as they were called – in its beak, the others dived to snatch it away, it fell on the beach, they all swooped down for it, then flew ahead to settle along the tide line, quarelling and mewing, just like large farmyard chickens – except for the dazzling cleanliness of their colours – snow-white, pearl-grey and jet black.

'Is it a good year for fish?' Hari asked.

'The season's just started – we hope it will be good,' Lila said.

Then, in a low voice, hardly liking to ask a question of which he feared the answer, Hari asked, 'Did they find the fishing boats that were lost in the storm?'

'Did you hear about that?' they asked, amazed, then told him about the search party that had gone out, led by Biju's powerful new boat, and brought them home, battered but alive – except for three men from Alibagh who had drowned.

'So Biju's boat was of some use after all,' Hari said with relief. He felt almost as if he himself had been dragged out of a stormy sea on to a placid shore.

'It is a wonderful boat,' Bela and Kamal chorused, but Lila said, 'Still, he need not boast about it all the time.'

'No, but we have to be thankful if he saved the fishermen,' Hari reminded her. He felt deeply grateful himself and told the girls how he had heard the news on the radio during the storm and how he had longed to come home to Thul and be with his own people again. It had made him realize he was a Thul boy and would always be one, he told them, which made them beam with joy.

The fishing fleet was trying to come in, the sails outlined against the sky like fins. As the tide was going out, the boats had to drop anchor at sea and the fisherwomen had to wade out to them with their saris tucked up, to receive the loaded baskets from the fishermen and carry them back to shore. A great screaming and haggling went up as the baskets were brought in and uncovered.

'They make more noise than the gulls,' said Lila.

'Shall we buy some? I have money,' Hari said proudly.

'Oh, you have come back rich from the city, have you?' the girls teased, laughing and pleased.

'Rich for a few days, at least,' said Hari. 'Come, choose, Lila. Buy a pomfret, or a *surmai*, or some crabs.'

But Lila was not used to being rich, even for a day. She stood watching the others bargain and haggle and after all the baskets of prawns and pomfrets had been sold, she bought some *jaola*, the minute whiskery shrimps that crawled at the bottom of a bag in a pink, pulpy mass and were the cheapest fish one could buy. Bela and Kamal were disappointed but Hari said, 'I have not eaten *jaola* for so long,' and Lila tied up her purchase in a bundle to take home.

Before they turned homewards, they walked as far as the creek that separated Thul from the Alibagh beach. The smaller, lighter craft were drawn up the creek, their sails lowered but their banners, made from long strips of fisherwomen's saris, fluttering and flying in the wind. Beyond them the sere brown hills were turning to bronze and purple against the golden sky.

Hari and his sisters walked down to the mouth of the creek where the sea had brought in banks of shells with every wave that swept over the sandbar. Most of them were crushed to a grainy, glittering powder but there were a few large chunks that gleamed with mother-of-pearl on the insides. Hari bent to pick them up and hurl them into the sea. Across the creek was the casuarina grove of Alibagh beach and beyond that the town and the fort, built long ago by the Angres, the great sea warriors of Moghul days.

Looking across at Alibagh, Lila said, 'Tomorrow is Diwali. Tomorrow we are to go and bring Mother home.'

'Can she come home to stay now? Is she quite well?'

'Much better. The doctor said he would let her go home at Diwali.'

'Then I will go and fetch her.'

'Yes, you can go in the morning while the girls and I get everything ready for Diwali.'

'Let's go home and eat,' cried Bela, suddenly very hungry.

'Run – I'll race you,' shouted Hari and they set off, shouting.

The horizon was brightly lit by the sun that seemed to be melting into the sea like a globe of molten glass. The sky had paled to lemon-yellow and in the east it was already mauve. A star appeared, the brilliant evening star that was always the first to shine.

At last Hari dropped back, panting, to walk at Lila's side.

'When we get home, you'll have to tell us all about Bombay,' Lila said.

'But first you must tell me all the news of home,' said Hari.

So after they had eaten, they left the lantern burning in the hut and sat outside under the stars where the fireflies floated like luminous fishes through the damp darkness of the coconut grove and the marsh. Then they talked and talked of all that had happened in the months that they had been apart.

After Hari had told them all about the Sri Krishna Eating House and the Ding Dong Watchworks and Mr Panwallah and Jagu and the park and Coconut Day, it was Lila's turn to tell him what had happened in his absence.

'All the time we waited for you, I thought you would come home for Diwali,' she ended.

'And you did,' cried Kamal, hugging Hari's arm and making the new bangles on her wrists jingle and flash as she did so.

'Of course,' said Hari, patting her hand. 'And tomorrow is Diwali and I'm going to Alibagh to see Mother –'

'And bring her home, *please*,' begged Bela.

'Of course,' Hari promised. He smiled at her, at all of them. 'You're all wonderful,' he said. 'It's wonderful how you've managed all these months – so well.'

Lila couldn't help smiling a little proud smile then. 'We managed,' she said, and then looked down at her feet in shyness. 'No, we couldn't have managed alone – the de Silvas helped Mother, and Sayyid Ali Sahib at the bungalow helped us after all the others left. We couldn't have managed alone.'

'Sayyid Ali Sahib?' Hari frowned. The name sounded familiar but he couldn't remember where he had heard it before: in Bombay, or had the girls mentioned it earlier? Feeling curious about the stranger in the bungalow, he said, 'After I come back from Alibagh, I'll go and thank him for looking after all of you.'

'No,' said Bela loudly. 'We looked after ourselves – and him, too.'

'Yes, you did,' Hari agreed, smiling. 'You are wonderful, all of you.'

13

O N DIWALI morning, Hari left his sisters to their preparations and set off down the village road to catch a bus to Alibagh. He had asked Lila what he could buy for her and bring back but she only shook her head and said, 'We already have all we need, Hari.' But when he set off down the sandy path through the coconut grove, Bela came running after him, caught him by the elbow and whispered, 'Hari, will you get us some of those sugar toys that they sell in Alibagh at Diwali? You know what I mean – those white sugar horses and elephants? I have some money that Sayyid Ali Sahib gave me when I pulled him out of the water –'

'If you did that to earn some money, you must keep it,' laughed Hari. 'I will buy you the sugar toys with *my* money,' he said proudly and went striding away.

It was a golden morning of the kind you get when the monsoon is over, the dampness and the moist haze are drying and lifting, and the coming winter casts dew on the grass and brings freshness to the air. Hari skirted their field and stood at one corner for a while, staring at it and wondering how he would set out a poultry farm on it. He knew nothing about chickens but perhaps he could learn, it would not be too difficult. He would just buy a few chickens to start with and then increase the size of the farm as he learned more about them and became more confident. That would keep them going till the factory came up, and the housing colony, when he could start off as the village watchmender.

The thought made him feel cheerful and optimistic and he turned off into the village road and marched on down the muddy track between the coconut and the betel palms, glad to see the old houses still exactly the same, the old men sitting on the swings on their verandas and the women painting *rangoli* designs on the tiles for Diwali and hanging paper lanterns in the doorways while chickens scratched and cats dozed in the shady yards. At the end of the road the pond was still beautiful with pink and white lotuses in bloom and women stood beating their washing on flat stones on the bank. Then the road became more rutted and dusty as it wound past the girls' school and the boys' school to the little brown hill at the crossing of the village road and the highway where he hoped to catch a bus.

He was watching a pair of kites wheeling and tumbling in the cobalt blue sky above the temple on the hill when a cycle came along, tinkling its bell madly, and Ramu flew off the seat and stood before him, shouting, 'Hari! Hari's back! Where did you go, Hari? When did you come back?'

Hari laughed at the amount of noise Ramu always managed to make all by himself. 'I was in Bombay, Ramu.'

'Are you going back already?'

'No, I'm going to Alibagh to see my mother at the hospital.'

'I'm going to Alibagh, too, to buy fireworks for Diwali. Come, sit, I'll take you.'

Hari jumped on at the back and Ramu pedalled off. The old rusty bicycle made such a noise as it bumped along that it hardly seemed possible to talk to each other, but they shouted what they had to say and managed to catch most of it above the clatter of the machine.

'When did you come?'

'Yesterday. For Diwali.'

'Going back after Diwali?'

'No, I think I'll stay. I made some money – I've brought it back. I'll try and work here now.'

'Work here?' jeered Ramu in his old manner. 'What work can you find here?'

'I'll do something,' Hari shouted cheerfully, keeping things to himself.

'You can't work on your own,' shouted Ramu. 'Wait for the factory to come up, then there'll be jobs.'

'I thought the fishermen and farmers of Alibagh were going to stop it from coming up.'

'Hah! That's what you went to Bombay for, wasn't it, to stop the government from building it? How can a few villagers stop the government from building it? How can a few villagers stop the government?'

Hari was silent and listened to Ramu as he went on shouting in his usual fashion: 'Everything has to change over here – everything is going to be different.'

'But, Ramu,' interrupted Hari at last, '*we* have to change too, *we* shall have to become different as well.'

That silenced Ramu and Hari held on to the bicycle seat and looked about him at the muddy fields and the bullock carts that were dragging ploughs through them, getting them ready for the sowing of the winter crops. He could not imagine this scene changed or this life coming to an end.

Then they were in Alibagh, the big town of the district, with its whitewashed bungalows, its wide roads, markets and shops where you could get mill-made bread, fireworks, anything you wanted. Hari got off the bicycle and went in search of sugar toys for his sisters after waving goodbye to Ramu who waved back silently, looking thoughtful as he took in all the changes that had come about in Hari. After buying a bagful from a barrow on the pavement, Hari walked straight up the road to the hospital gates.

He was standing in the yard, looking about him, searching for someone in hospital uniform

whom he could ask about his mother, when an
old man shuffled across to him, put a trembling
hand on his elbow and muttered, 'Hari, is it you?'

Hari gaped at the wrinkled face and the grey
matted hair for a whole minute before he gasped,
'Father!'

'You have come to see her?' the old man
quavered. 'You have come at last?'

'I was in Bombay, Father –'

'And you never came once to see her?'

'I came back yesterday. Lila told me she was
here. Can I take her home now?'

'You must go and ask the doctor-sahib that,'
the old man said, pointing down the long veranda
to a room at the end that was curtained with
green cloth at the door. Hari went slowly towards
it and, holding the curtain aside, looked in. There
was a doctor sitting at the table and writing busily
and some nurses at the other end of the room,
washing up at the sink and cleaning things. They
looked at Hari and called over the doctor's head,
'What is it? What do you want?'

Hari murmured his mother's name, wondering if they would know her. They did,
instantly. After all, she had been with them for
seven months.

'Yes, yes, yes – go and see her – ward two, bed forty-five,' shouted a large nurse with friendly eyes that gleamed behind her spectacles.

Then the doctor stopped writing and looked at him. 'Who are you? Are you from her village?'

'I am her son, from – from Bombay,' Hari had to say in order to explain why he had not been there before.

'Oh, from Bombay? No one told me she had a son in Bombay,' said the doctor. 'I only saw the daughter, from Thul. Come to fetch her home for Diwali, have you?'

Hari nodded, watching the doctor's face to see if this were possible.

'Yes,' the doctor nodded. 'She is strong enough to go home. But you must bring her back for a check-up every month. We can't let her go back to the hands of your village quack. She has recovered and we have to make sure she stays well.'

'I will bring her back,' Hari promised eagerly. 'I am not going back to Bombay. I will stay here now, in my village, and I will bring her back every month.'

'See that you do,' said the doctor, 'for she still needs looking after,' and then he turned and spoke to the nurse about the discharge papers. When all the papers were ready, signed and in order, Hari was taken to the ward at last.

He could hardly recognize his mother. For a long time he had seen her only lying in bed, half asleep, not speaking, and he could not believe that this woman sitting on the edge of her bed and smiling at him could be her. It was as if the years of illness had rolled up and disappeared, leaving her as she was before her illness. Of course her hair was grey now and her face lined, but she had put on weight and her eyes were bright.

'Hari! Hari! Have you come home for Diwali?'

'Yes, I've come to take you home for Diwali.'

'Can I?' she turned to ask the nurse eagerly.

'Of course – we are not going to keep you in hospital at Diwali. It's time you went home to your children,' said the nurse. 'Come, let's pack your things – your clothes, your comb, your medicines –'

And in a little while Hari and his father were helping her into a tonga they had hired at the gate. She was weak in her legs, quite unused to walking, and trembled with nervousness at being out on the street in the bright light, but Hari and his father sat on either side of her on the broad back seat of the tonga and held her arms so she would not slip off. Then the tonga driver flicked his whip over the horse's back and it set off at a trot, carrying them home to Thul for Diwali.

Lila, Bela and Kamal had everything ready by the time they arrived home. A *rangoli* had been drawn on the veranda floor with coloured powders, yellow and magenta and white, and a big red paper lantern hung from the beams, its streamers rustling in the wind. In the house, all the brass cooking pots and tumblers had been polished till they shone like lamps on the kitchen shelf, and Lila had arranged all the festive sweets on a tray – fried dumplings stuffed with shredded coconut and semolina, round yellow balls made of gram flour and sugar, chunks of crystallized pumpkin and marrow, squares of thick cream cooked with nuts and raisins – and she was frying bright orange squiggly *jalebis* in a pan of hot oil and dropping them into a bowl of syrup when Hari arrived with their parents.

Bela and Kamal had garlands ready for their mother, made of jasmine, roses and marigolds, and they cried and laughed as they put them over her head. To their dismay it was their father who started crying weakly at the scene while their mother laughed with joy. She went straight to the small altar in a corner of the kitchen where there were small clay idols of Ganesha and the goddess Lakshmi standing amidst sticks of incense and piles of rose petals, and offered them the garland with a prayer of thanksgiving.

In the evening Hari helped his sisters to arrange the little clay lamps in rows along the veranda, on the low walls, the paths and around the trees and shrubs of the garden. Lila poured a little oil into each carefully, Bela and Kamal laid a cottonwool wick in the oil, dipping one end down into it and then squeezing it dry between their fingers so it would light when Hari came around with a candle. In the dark, the golden lights flowered to life and gleamed.

Then Hari carried the basket of fireworks on to the grassy knoll in the coconut grove and, to the sound of Beja's and Kamal's excited shrieks, he set off a rocket into the sky where it exploded with a bang into a shower of coloured sparks. The girls came running forwards to light sparklers at a candle he held for them, then ran around the coconut grove, waving them in the air so that they left patterns of light in the velvety darkness. Then Lila lit a 'pomegranate', bending with a candle to set fire to a clay pot with its little mouth papered with silver foil, and it exploded into a fountain of gold and silver stars that shot up almost as high as the coconut trees and then fell to earth in a shower. Bela and Kamal lit Catherine wheels on the smooth surface of the veranda floor where they whirled around dizzily, sending off white-hot sparks, and Hari jumped over them and kicked them about to make them change course while Lila and his mother begged him to be careful. So he went out to the knoll and set off more rockets, waiting for each to shoot across the sky like a comet and explode with a bang into a cloud of stars before he set off the next.

When they had finished the fireworks in the basket and Bela and Kamal said sadly, 'Oh, they are all finished already,' Hari said, 'Now let's go out on the beach and light a bonfire,' so they laughed and clapped their hands and ran after him down the dark path to the beach, Hari showing them the way with a lighted torch made out of a dry coconut branch. Lila stayed on the veranda with her parents, saying, 'We will watch from here – it's too windy on the beach for Ma.'

Hari and Bela and Kamal knelt on the cold sand and stacked dry coconut branches carefully, making a pyramid of them. Then Hari set fire to it and they stood back from the crackling flames and watched the dry fronds and branches burn swiftly till the whole pyramid collapsed into ashes and embers. Now the darkness of the night crept over them – sky, sand and sea were all black velvet, deep and soft, into which they sank. But once their eyes grew accustomed to it they could make out the white line of the surf as it came whispering out of the sea towards them, the phosphorescence that gave a ghostly glow to the waves and the pale gleam of the sand. Of course the sky was illuminated with millions and millions of stars that burnt brilliantly and silently above them.

'Come, let's go back and sit with Ma,' said Hari when the last of the burning branches had collapsed with a sigh into ashes and embers.

'And Ma will tell us the Diwali story,' Bela said, suddenly remembering a custom they had observed for years and that she recalled from her infancy.

So they went back to the veranda, still lit by the rosy paper lantern, and sat at their mother's feet while she told them the story of Diwali, of how Rama, the prince of Ayodhya, had fought a great battle with Ravana, the demon-king of Lanka, to win back his wife Sita who had been kidnapped in a forest, and how, victorious, they had returned to Ayodhya to find the whole city lit up to receive them.

'And that is why we light up our houses on Diwali, too,' sighed Bela, remembering the line with which their mother had always ended the story.

'Yes,' she said, 'and the lights will show the way to Lakshmi who is the goddess of wealth so that she will visit our house too and not miss it in the dark.'

'It is Hari-*bhai* who has brought us wealth, Mother,' said Kamal seriously, patting Hari's arm and making him glow with pride.

'I feel wealthy when I see all of you beside me,' said their mother quietly.

There was a little silence as they sat listening to the wind in the palms and the surf breaking on the beach and watching the lamps flicker and the stars shine. Then their father coughed, cleared his throat and spoke for the first time in his rusty voice. 'Only our Pinto is missing,' he said, making them all start with surprise. 'Poor Pinto,' he murmured, and fell silent again. Although he said no more, everyone realized he was saying he was sorry for the role he had played in Pinto's death, for being responsible for it in a way. It was the first time he had ever said he was sorry for the way things had been in the past. They were all struck dumb till Lila got up, wiping her eyes with a corner of her sari, and said, as if to console her father, 'Shall I make you some tea? Or would you like hot milk?'

He shook his head and so did the others: they wanted nothing more now.

The day after Diwali was the Hindu New Year's Day when every house in the village was decorated with fresh garlands of mango leaves and marigolds, every shop opened a new ledger at a special ceremony and prayers were said to Lakshmi, the goddess of wealth, in the hope that she would bless them in the coming new year.

So the next morning found Lila and her sisters busily sweeping and cleaning and putting up fresh garlands and drawing new *rangoli* patterns. Later in the day the annual bullock cart races were to be held on the beach and excitement ran high in the village where bullocks were having their curved horns painted pink for the occasion while the tonga drivers decked their tongas with tinsel and streamers and brushed and curried their horses and brightened their harnesses with spangles.

Only Hari had nothing to do. He watched the others for a while and then said, 'There's nothing for me to do now so I'll go and visit the sahib up at the house.'

'All right, but come back soon,' called his mother who was sitting on the veranda floor and helping Lila to draw an elaborate *rangoli*.

'You said you would take us to the races on the beach, Hari,' his younger sisters screamed when they saw him crossing the log over the creek.

'I know, I know,' he called. 'I'll be back on time.'

When he went up to *Mon Repos* he found Lila had already swept it clean and drawn a simple red and white *rangoli* pattern on the veranda tiles while the younger girls had hung a garland of mango leaves over the door. There was no one there now and it was very quiet. Hari had to wander around and search before he found the sahib down at the edge of the marsh, sitting amongst the rushes, as still as the heron on the stone, staring through his binoculars at the coconut tree on the other bank.

He heard Hari's footsteps and turned his head slightly but did not speak. Hari hesitated, wondering where he had seen the man before. He searched his crowded memories of Bombay for a hint because that was where the man had come from, his sisters had told him, but he could not remember.

'Am I disturbing you, sir? Shall I come later?' he asked uncertainly.

In answer the gentleman patted the ground beside him and said, 'Do you want to talk to me? Sit down – then we won't disturb the birds.'

Hari knew from his sisters that the sahib was 'studying the birds' but he had no idea how one did such a thing. Now he would learn: Mr Panwallah had told him he must go on and on learning whatever he could and never stop.

Remembering that, it struck him how like Mr Panwallah this gentleman was although he had white hair under his beret and a beard. Both of them were somehow birdlike. It made him feel confident and reassured enough to ask respectfully, 'You are studying the birds here, sir?'

'I have been studying the nest-building habits of the baya birds,' said the gentleman and waved his hand at the nests that dangled and swayed from the coconut tree that leaned across the marsh. 'I watched them all through the monsoon and now they are bringing up their young, see,' he said in a tone of excitement and turned away from Hari to watch.

Hari had no alternative but to watch, too, although he had never paid the birds any attention before. They were not even pretty birds like the kingfishers or egrets, but small and spotted and brown like sparrows, although some had yellow heads. But now that he was forced to look, it struck Hari how wonderful it was that these small creatures had built this colony of strange nests that swung above the water where no one could get at them and harm the young. The nests were shaped like tubes or funnels, and woven neatly out of grasses and paddy leaves, made compact by careful weaving and blobs of mud. The birds flew in and out of them, crying, 'Tililili, tililee – kiti – tililee – kitee.'

The gentleman explained to Hari, 'It is so difficult to build a nest like that that the young male has to practise before he actually plans to build one and raise a family. If anything goes wrong and the nest does not turn out right, he abandons it and starts another. It is only when the nest is perfect that he is satisfied. And he builds several so that he can have several wives. He even decorates them by sticking on flower petals or feathers with blobs of mud to attract the females. Females will only mate with those that have managed to build them good homes.' He chuckled. 'Can you think of anything cleverer?'

Suddenly Hari gave a start: he recognized the voice, he was sure he had heard it before. He turned and stared at the man in wonder, and then realized who it was – the man who had spoken to the crowds at the Black Horse in Bombay and told them why he, a citizen of Bombay, cared so deeply for the Alibagh coast and feared so much that it would be spoilt by all the changes that were to come. Now here he was, in Thul!

'Sir,' he blurted out, 'sir, I heard you speak at the Black Horse, in Bombay, when I came with the men from my village –'

The gentleman lowered his binoculars and stared at him as a bird might, with his head a little to one side. 'Oh, you were one of them?' he asked, and at last seemed to find Hari as interesting as one of his weaver birds. 'I see, I see. Come let us go into the veranda and talk – it is too damp to sit here for long.'

But even when he was on the veranda he could not give up his binoculars and his observation of birds and kept raising them to his eyes to watch the flight of a drongo or some bee eaters with little chuckles of delight which made Hari feel that he had missed a great deal by paying no attention to the birds that swarmed in Thul. He would have to learn to use his eyes more, he decided, when the gentleman lowered his binoculars and said, 'So, you're one of the Alibagh farmers who came to Bombay to give a petition to the chief minister, are you?'

'Oh no, sir, I'm from Thul – I live in that hut there,' Hari told him. 'My sisters wash and cook for you.'

'Ah yes, yes,' he cried, but just then a pair of fork-tailed drongoes swooped into the air and somersaulted in the sunlight, making their blue-black feathers glint, and he gave a cry and stared open-mouthed at them.

'I went to Bombay in the procession,' Hari reminded him, interrupting the harsh shrieks of the drongoes. 'We wanted to stop them from building a factory here.'

'Ahh,' sighed the birdwatcher, dropping the binoculars and sinking down into a cane chair. 'So you're one of those who put up a fight. You've lost the fight, you know – we lost the case in court. The politicians won – so they can make plenty of money from the sale of land and licences in the name of progress. Thul is lost,' he sighed, straightening the spectacles on his nose. 'Everything is doomed. The fish in the sea will die from the effluents that will be pumped into the water. The paddy fields will be built over by factories and houses and streets. My little baya birds will find no more paddy leaves for their nests. Or grain or food for their young.

They will have to fly away. I may not see them another year.'

He sounded so heartbroken that Hari asked, 'Why do you care so much about the birds, sir?'

'The birds are the last free creatures on earth. Everything else has been captured and tamed and enslaved – tigers behind the bars of the zoos, lions stared at by crowds in safari parks, men and women in houses like matchboxes working in factories that are like prisons. Only the birds are free and can take off and fly away into space when they like.' His face shone when he spoke and his voice trembled. 'I suppose that is why I love them – for their freedom, which we don't have. Perhaps I would also like to leave all – all this ugliness we've made on earth and fly with them. Wouldn't you?' he asked Hari.

'But we can't fly, sir,' Hari reminded him, earnestly. 'We are here on earth, we cannot leave it. We must live here, somehow.'

The gentleman looked at him with sad eyes. 'Yes, what will you do? What will become of you? I don't know, my friend. When it comes to people, I – I know nothing. I am lost. What will you do?'

Hari came a little closer to him. 'Sir, I thought – I thought – since it is too late to start fishing or

farming now, this will not be a good place to farm
or fish any more, and since I don't want to work
in a factory – I thought I would buy some chickens,
build chicken coops in my field, start a poultry
farm, sell eggs in the village and chickens to the
rich people who will come to Thul once the
factory is built, and so we will live – for a while.
Later I want to set up a watchmending shop – I
have learnt a little watchmending,' he added with
shy pride.

'Have you?' asked the birdwatcher in astonishment. 'Can you – d'you think you can mend
my watch for me? I fell into the creek, you know,'
he chuckled, 'and my watch hasn't worked since.
Do you think you can get it to tick?' He took it
out of his shirt pocket and handed it to Hari who
took it eagerly. He could hardly believe that he
was being asked to do something for the great
man who had spoken to him in Bombay and
come to Thul to study the birds.

Taking the watch, he shook it gently and held it
to his ear. 'Water has got into the works, sir. It is
very easy to clean and dry that – I did many
during the monsoon in Bombay.'

The birdwatcher was staring at him as he spoke
as if he were a bird performing some wonderful

and interesting act. Then he shot out of his chair, crying, 'Adapt! Adapt!'

'What, sir?' asked Hari, puzzled. He did not know the word.

'Adapt – that is what you are going to do. Just as birds and animals must do if they are going to survive. Just like the sparrows and pigeons that have adapted themselves to city life and live on food leftovers and rubbish thrown to them in the streets instead of searching for grain and insects in the fields,' he explained, 'so you will have to adapt to your new environment.'

I don't think I know how to do that, sir,' said Hari uncertainly.

'But, boy, you've just told me how you are going to do it. You are going to give up your traditional way of living and learn a new way to suit the new environment that the factory will create at Thul so as to survive. Yes, you will survive.'

Hari could not understand half the words the birdwatcher was using. He could not understand him at all but his words reminded him of what Mr Panwallah had said to him the day he went to see him and found him sitting on his balcony and watching the pigeons on the station roof 'The wheel turns,' he said slowly and wonderingly, remembering Mr Panwallah's words. 'The wheel turns and turns and turns,' he said, understanding, and turned to tell Sayyid Ali that he understood the connection now, and how birds and men were united in this great turning of the wheel, and how the birds, if we understood them, could show us and teach us many important things. 'Sir, I understand,' he shouted, but just then the excited figure of the birdwatcher suddenly stopped hopping about on the edge of the veranda and disappeared abruptly: he had tumbled backwards and fallen off the veranda into the hibiscus bush below. Hari jumped down to help him to his feet, asking anxiously, 'Are you hurt, sir? Are you all right, sir?'

'Yes, yes, yes,' stammered the birdwatcher who only seemed a little shaken and began to chuckle as Hari helped him dust his clothes and find his binoculars. 'It's a good thing I'd given you my watch,' he laughed, 'or I'd have broken that, too.'

'It's safe with me, sir,' Hari said, patting his pocket, 'and I'll take it home and fix it so I can give it back to you by this evening. Will that be all right, sir?'

But the birdwatcher did not reply: with a cry of delight, he was stumbling back to the marsh, having seen a little baya bird arrive with something in its beak for its young. He seemed to have forgotten Hari.

Hari did not really mind: what the birdwatcher had told him had already filled him with the confidence he needed and wanted. Now he would go ahead.

Of course he would first take his sisters to the races on the beach.

Their horns painted pink and crimson, the milk-white bullocks thundered over the sand, the wooden carts lumbering after them, the drivers in their bright new turbans shouting themselves hoarse as they waved their whips in the air and urged them along.

'Biju's cart – Biju's bullocks – Biju's won!' A shout went up at the far end of the beach and was passed back through the crowds on the dunes. Biju, standing amongst them in a new, dazzling white *dhoti*, beamed, looking larger and broader than ever, with his wife and daughter beside him in their new Diwali finery. People shouted and congratulated him – they seemed to have forgiven

Biju at last for his boasting and arrogance – after all, he had helped to rescue the drowning fishermen. That great storm had brought all the fishermen closer together, they had realized how much they depended on each other and needed each other, and they seemed to be celebrating this closeness today.

Then it was the turn of the tongas which were lighter and went faster, the wheels spinning over the sand and the horses flying along, their necks outstretched, their manes rippling and the spangles on their harnesses glinting.

'Look, look, look,' screamed Bela and Kamal, beside themselves with excitement.

'Don't scream,' said Hari. 'Here, have some sweets,' he added, and passed them the bag of sugar toys he had bought for them in Alibagh. The girls fell upon them and munched loudly and happily after passing them around to their friends. Life seemed perfect to them at that moment.

After the races, when the crowds had thinned, Hari still stood on the dunes and saw a group of women coming down the path with small flat baskets on the palms of their hands. They were walking down the beach to the three rocks that stood in the sea. He watched them wade into the peacock blue and green sea, the foam breaking against their ankles, to scatter flower petals and coloured powder on the rocks as they prayed to the sea. He saw that his mother was amongst them.

'Lila, look!' he said. 'Look, Lila.'

1937   *Anita Desai (née Mazumbar) is born in Mussoorie, northern India*

1957   *Graduates from Delhi university with a BA in English literature*

1958   *Marries businessman Ashvin Desai; they have four children together*

1963   *Her first book* Cry, the Peacock *is published*

1978   *Receives both the Winifred Holtby Memorial Prize and the National Academy of Letters Award for her novel* Fire on the Mountain

1980   *Shortlisted for the Booker Prize for fiction, and again in 1994 and 1999*

1982   *A Village by the Sea is first published*

1983   *Awarded the Guardian Children's Fiction Prize for* The Village by the Sea

1993   *Novel* In Custody *is adapted for screen*

1999   Fasting, Feasting *shortlisted for the Booker Prize for Fiction*

2005   The Zig Zag Way *is published*

2014   *Lives in the Hudson River Valley in the USA, travels to India and Mexico*

INTERESTING FACTS

Anita Desai was brought up speaking German at home but also learnt Hindi and English. As well as moving around in India she has lived in England and all over America.

She knew she wanted to write from a very young age; she read a lot of books and was found scribbling away in the corner of a room so often that her family called her 'The Writer'.

WHERE DID THE
STORY COME FROM?

*When her children were small, Anita Desai lived in
Mumbai and often took them to a small fishing village
on the Arabian Sea for holidays. There they observed
the lives of fishermen and rice and coconut famers,
but when the village was chosen as the site for a giant
fertilizer factory, much was to change. A poor family
that lived in a hut behind the big house went through
these changes. The book is about the ways in which
their lives were affected. Many families and many
places in India have had this experience.*

GUESS WHO?

A *She herself looked like a crumpled grey rag lying there. She had been ill for a long time.*

B *[He] was small and furry, grey and white, and brave as a lion*

C *... the man who stood at the counter, wearing a small black cap and with an eyepiece fixed to his eye, working at a minute watch that he held in the cup of his hand*

WORDS GLORIOUS WORDS!

Lots of words have several different meanings – here are a few you'll find in this Puffin book. Use a **dictionary** or look them up online to find other definitions.

inundated *overwhelmed by things that need attention*

dhoti *a garment worn by men in India*

arid *a region suffering from immensely dry soil, often barren*

jalebi *a sweet made from sugar, flour and water*

dissipate *to get rid of or cause something to disappear*

taciturn *someone who says little; reserved*

puja *a religious ceremony involving prayer*

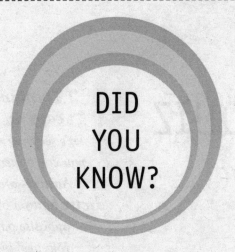

DID YOU KNOW?

Bombay is no longer known by that name; it was renamed **Mumbai** in 1996. Mumbai is the second most densely populated city in India, after the capital Delhi, and is among the top *most populated* cities in the world. Alarmingly, more than *fifty per cent* of Mumbai's population *lives in slums* like Jagu and his family.

Thul is the name of a real village on the Western coast of India. There are many places in India, and across the world, *suspended* between tradition and modernity, grappling to come to terms with *change.*

MR PANWALLAH SAYS:
'Learn, learn, learn – so that you can grow and change. Things change all the time, boy – nothing remains the same [. . .] The wheel turns and turns: it never stops and stands still.'

QUIZ

Thinking caps on – let's see how much you can remember! Answers are at the bottom of the opposite page. (No peeking!)

1 *What is the name of Biju's new boat?*

a) Seagull

b) Mermaid

c) Starfish

d) Sky

2 *What does Lila give to the medicine man for payment?*

a) *a ring*

b) *a bangle*

c) *money*

d) *food*

3 *What does the elderly man, Sayyid Ali Sahib, study whilst staying at Mon Repos?*

a) *plants*

b) *rocks*

c) *birds*

d) *insects*

4 *Where does Hari normally sleep when he's living in Bombay?*

a) *on the street*

b) *in a hotel*

c) *in the slums*

d) *in the park*

5 *During which celebration does Mr Panwallah take Hari to the beach in Bombay?*

a) *Holi*

b) *Diwali*

c) *Coconut Day*

d) *Onam*

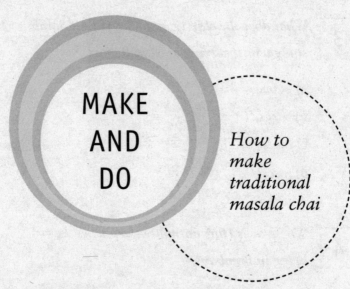

MAKE AND DO

How to make traditional masala chai

During the course of this story we hear about the characters cradling a cup of sweet, fragrant and nourishing tea; unlike our tea, this is spiced, creamy and sweetened, and referred to as 'chai' (a word meaning 'tea' in many parts of the world). It is a centuries-old drink and is an important part of Indian quotidian culture. There are many different customs and variations so try playing around with different spices (such as star anise) and, if you like the taste, try making chai milkshakes or even chai ice cream!

These ingredients will make enough for one cup of masala chai. This recipe will use whole fat milk but you can use almond, soya milk or even trying adding a little cream.

YOU WILL NEED:

* 180ml water plus 60ml milk
* 2 heaped teaspoons of loose black tea
  (preferably Assam or Ceylon)
* 2 green cardamom pods (cracked)
* 4 whole cloves
* 2–3 whole black peppercorns
* 1/4 teaspoon fennel seeds
* 1–2 cinnamon sticks
* Fresh ginger (2–3 thin slices)
* Sweetener (unrefined sugar or honey is best)

1 Place the cardamom pods, cloves, peppercorns, fennel seeds and cinnamon into a pestle and mortar and grind into a powder.

2 Add your ground spices to the water in a saucepan and bring the mixture to the boil. Cover, turn to a low heat and simmer for 10 minutes.

3 Add the milk and sugar and bring the mixture to a simmer again.

4 Then add the loose black tea and the fresh ginger, turn off the heat and allow this infusion to steep for 2 minutes.

5 Pour into a cup through a sieve to strain out tea leaves and spices.

6 Enjoy!

IN THIS YEAR

1982 Fact Pack

What else was happening in the world when this Puffin book was published?

The **Falklands War** is a ten-week long battle between Britain and Argentina.

Prince William is born in June, in Paddington, London

The film **E.T.** is released and tops the charts. Meanwhile, Michael Jackson's album **Thriller** tops the music charts for the final months of 1982.

Diet Coke is introduced.

PUFFIN WRITING TIP

Like Hari, change your scenery and go see something you've never seen before.

Anita surrounds herself with memories; she has photographs, shells and fragments collected throughout her life. Try looking at your old family photos – as well as embarrassing haircuts you might find out something you never knew!

If you have enjoyed *The Village by the Sea* you may like to read *Chinese Cinderella* by Adeline Yen Mah, the true story of an unwanted daughter.

1. Top of the Class
全 班 考 第 一

Autumn, 1941

AS SOON as I got home from school, Aunt Baba noticed the silver medal dangling from the left breast-pocket of my uniform. She was combing her hair in front of the mirror in our room when I rushed in and plopped my school-bag down on my bed.

'What's that hanging on your dress?'

'It's something special that Mother Agnes gave me in front of the whole class this afternoon. She called it an award.'

My aunt looked thrilled. 'So soon? You only started kindergarten one week ago. What is it for?'

'It's for topping my class this week. When Mother Agnes pinned it on my dress, she said I could wear it for seven days. Here, this certificate goes with it.' I opened my school-bag and handed her an envelope as I climbed onto her lap.

She opened the envelope and took out the certificate.

'Why, it's all written in French or English or some other foreign language. How do you expect me to read this, my precious little treasure?' I knew she was pleased because she was smiling as she hugged me. 'One day soon,' she continued, 'you'll be able to translate all this into Chinese for me. Until then, we'll just write today's date on the envelope and put it away somewhere safe. Go close the door properly and put on the latch so no one will come in.'

I watched her open her closet door and take out her safe-deposit box. She took the key from a gold chain around her neck and placed my certificate underneath her jade bracelet, pearl necklace and diamond watch – as if my award were also some precious jewel impossible to replace.

As she closed the lid, an old photograph fell out. I picked up the faded picture and saw a solemn young man and woman, both dressed in old-fashioned Chinese robes. The man looked rather familiar.

'Is this a picture of my father and dead mama?' I asked.

'No. This is the wedding picture of your grandparents. Your Ye Ye was twenty-six and your Nai Nai was only fifteen.' She quickly took the photo from me and locked it in her box.

'Do you have a picture of my dead mama?'

She avoided my eyes. 'No. But I have wedding pictures of your father and stepmother Niang. You were only one year old when they married. Do you want to see them?'

'No. I've seen those before. I just want to see one of my own mama. Do I look like her?' Aunt Baba did not reply, but busied herself putting the safe-deposit box back into her closet. After a while I said, 'When did my mama die?'

'Your mother came down with a high fever three days after you were born. She died when you were two weeks old . . .' She hesitated for a moment, then exclaimed suddenly, 'How dirty your hands are! Have you been playing in that sand-box at school again? Go wash them at once! Then come back and do your homework!'

I did as I was told. Though I was only four years old, I understood I should not ask Aunt Baba too many questions about my dead mama. Big Sister once told me, 'Aunt Baba and Mama used to be best friends. A long time ago, they worked together in a bank in Shanghai owned by our Grand Aunt, the youngest sister of Grandfather Ye Ye. But then Mama died giving birth to you. If you had not been born, Mama would still be alive. She died because of you. You are bad luck.'

2. A Tianjin Family
天 津 家 庭

At the time of my birth, Big Sister was six and a half years old. My three brothers were five, four and three. They blamed me for causing Mama's (媽媽) death and never forgave me.

A year later, Father (爸爸) remarried. Our stepmother, whom we called Niang (娘), was a seventeen-year-old Eurasian beauty fourteen years his junior. Father always introduced her to his friends as his French wife though she was actually half French and half Chinese. Besides Chinese, she spoke French and English. She was almost as tall as Father, stood very straight and dressed only in French clothes – many of which came from Paris. Her thick, wavy, black hair never had a curl out of place. Her large, dark-brown eyes were fringed with long, thick lashes. She wore heavy make-up, expensive French perfume and many diamonds and pearls. It was Grandmother Nai Nai who told us to call her Niang, another Chinese term for 'mother'.

One year after their wedding, they had a son (Fourth Brother) followed by a daughter (Little Sister). There were now seven of us: five children from Father's first wife and two from our stepmother, Niang.

As well as Father and Niang, we lived with our Grandfather Ye Ye (爺爺), Grandmother Nai Nai (奶奶) and Aunt Baba (姑媽) in a big house in the French Concession of Tianjin, a city port on the north-east coast of China. Aunt Baba was the older sister of our father. Because she was meek, shy, unmarried and had no money of her own, my parents ordered her to take care of me. From an early age, I slept in a cot in her room. This suited me well because I grew to know her better and better and we came to share a life apart from the rest of our family. Under the circumstances, perhaps it was inevitable that, in time, we loved each other very deeply.

Many years before, China had lost a war (known as the Opium War) against England and France. As a result, many coastal cities in China (such as Tianjin and Shanghai) came to be occupied by foreign soldiers.

The conquerors parcelled out the best areas of these treaty ports for themselves, claiming them as their own 'territories' or 'concessions'. Tianjin's French Concession was like a little piece of Paris transplanted into the centre of this big Chinese city. Our house was built in the French style and looked as if it had been lifted from a tree-shaded avenue near the Eiffel Tower. Surrounded by a charming garden, it had porches, balconies, bow windows, awnings and a slanting tile roof. Across the street was St Louis Catholic Boys' School, where the teachers were French missionaries.

In December 1941, when the Japanese bombed Pearl Harbor, the United States became involved in the Second World War. Although Tianjin was occupied by the Japanese, the French Concession was still being governed by French officials. French policemen strutted about looking important and barking out orders in their own language, which they expected everyone to understand and obey.

At my school, Mother Agnes taught us the alphabet and how to count in French. Many of the streets around our house were named after dead French heroes or Catholic saints. When translated into Chinese, these street names became so complicated that Ye Ye and Nai Nai often had trouble remembering them. Bilingual store signs were common but the most exclusive shops painted their signs only in French. Nai Nai told us this was the foreigners' way of announcing that no Chinese were allowed there except for maids in charge of white children.

3. Nai Nai's Bound Feet
奶 奶 的 小 脚

THE DINNER-BELL rang at seven. Aunt Baba took my hand and led me into the dining-room.

My grandparents were just ahead of us. Aunt Baba told me to run quickly to the head of the big, round dining-table and pull out Grandmother Nai Nai's chair for her. Nai Nai walked very slowly because of her bound feet. I watched her as she inched her way towards me, hobbling and swaying as if her toes had been partly cut off. As she sat down with a sigh of relief, I placed my foot next to her embroidered, black-silk shoe to compare sizes.

'Nai Nai, how come your feet are so tiny?' I asked.

'When I was three years old, a tight bandage was wound around my feet, bending the toes under the sole and crushing the arch so that my feet would remain small all my life. This has been the custom in China for over one thousand years, ever since the Tang dynasty. In my day, small feet were considered feminine and beautiful. If you had large and unbound feet, no man would marry you. This was the custom.'

'Did it hurt?'

'Of course! It hurt so badly I couldn't sleep. I screamed with pain and begged my mother to free my feet but she wouldn't. In fact, the pain has never gone away. My feet have hurt every day since they were bound and continue to hurt today. I had a pair of perfectly normal feet when I was born, but they maimed me on purpose and gave me life-long arthritis so I would be attractive. Just be thankful this horrible custom was done away with thirty years ago. Otherwise your feet would be crippled and you wouldn't be able to run or jump either.'

I went to the foot of the table and sat at my assigned seat between Second Brother and Third

Brother as my three brothers ran in, laughing and jostling each other. I cringed as Second Brother sat down on my right. He was always saying mean things to me and grabbing my share of goodies when nobody was looking.

Second Brother used to sit next to Big Brother but the two of them fought a lot. Father finally separated them when they broke a fruit bowl fighting over a pear.

Big Brother winked at me as he sat down. He had a twinkle in his eye and was whistling a tune. Yesterday he'd tried to teach me how to whistle but no matter how hard I tried I couldn't make it work. Was Big Brother up to some new mischief today? Last Sunday afternoon, I came across him crouched by Grandfather Ye Ye's bed, watching him like a cat while Ye Ye took his nap. A long black hair from Ye Ye's right nostril was being blown out and drawn in with every snore. Silently but swiftly, Big Brother suddenly approached Ye Ye and carefully pinched the nasal hair between his forefinger and thumb. There was a tantalising pause as Ye Ye exhaled with a long, contented wheeze. Meanwhile I held my breath, mesmerised and not daring to make a sound. Finally, Ye Ye inhaled deeply. Doggedly, Big Brother hung on.

The hair was wrenched from its root. Ye Ye woke up with a yell, jumped from his bed, took in the situation with one glance and went after Big Brother with a feather duster. Laughing hysterically, Big Brother rushed out of the room, slid down the banister and made a clean getaway into the garden, all the time holding Ye Ye's hair aloft like a trophy.

Third Brother took his seat on my left. His lips were pursed and he was trying to whistle unsuccessfully. Seeing the medal on my uniform, he raised his eyebrow and smiled at me. 'What's that?' he asked.

'It's an award for topping my class. My teacher says I can wear it for seven days.'

'Congratulations! First week at school and you get a medal! Not bad!'

While I was basking in Third Brother's praise, I suddenly felt a hard blow across the back of my head. I turned around to see Second Brother glowering at me.